Max Fatchen

CLOSER TO THE STARS

Puffin Books

Puffin Books, Penguin Books Australia Ltd,
487 Maroondah Highway, P.O. Box 257
Ringwood, Victoria, 3134, Australia
Penguin Books Ltd,
Harmondsworth, Middlesex, England
Penguin Books,
40 West 23rd Street, New York, N.Y. 10010, U.S.A.
Penguin Books Canada Ltd,
2801 John Street, Markham, Ontario, Canada
Penguin Books (N.Z.) Ltd,
182-190 Wairau Road, Auckland 10, New Zealand

First published in Australia by Methuen Australia Pty Ltd, 1981
First published in Great Britain by Methuen Children's Books Ltd, 1981
Published by Penguin Books Australia, 1983
Copyright © Max Fatchen, 1981

Offset from Methuen hardback edition
Made and printed in Australia by
Dominion Press Hedges & Bell

CIP

Fatchen, Max
Closer to the stars.
First published simultaneously, Sydney & London: Methuen, 1981

For children
ISBN 0 14 031624 8.

I. Title.

A823'.3

Puffin Books

Closer to the Stars

1941 . . . and at the airforce base near Paul's farm, pilots are being trained for the war. Meanwhile they play games with their planes – barnstorming haystacks and frightening the townfolk – and then one of them becomes involved with Paul's sister, Nancy.

But when Nancy discovers she is pregnant, it is Paul who must help her confront the uncertain future, the hostile attitudes of small-town gossips . . . and the ultimate shattering blow.

Contents

For Harold

1. Haystacks at Six o'Clock

The hawk looked pinned to the sky as it hovered over the countryside, keeping its position with its tawny wings, its incredible eyes watching the movements on the ground below it.

There were the long lines of the roads, crisscrossing here and there, the brown paddocks dotted with brown sheep that trailed brown dust towards the water troughs.

Nearby the hangars and tin huts of an airfield caught the sun and small biplanes lifted into the morning with a distant roar, a sound that came and went as they took off, levelled out then throttled back their engines.

They didn't disturb the hawk because they were distant and it had become accustomed to them.

Its own small piece of air and ground was its concern; it was hungry and its hunger made it alert.

It kept its station well, although the warm currents lifting from the Australian plain made the bird rise, then in a quick dive it came back again, its wings fluttering and all its tidy and effective arrangement of feathers working to keep it where its instinct told it there might be prey below.

It was much more handsome than the noisy biplanes in the distance: it was designed as a predator with everything streamlined and arranged symmetrically for flight and sudden movement: with the fierce beak and strong talons and the watchful far-seeing eyes.

The little planes, too, were hawks in their way. Not that they had talons, only wheels that bumped and rolled on the grassy surface of the airstrip.

But the young men in them were training for war; for bigger, faster and deadlier planes, engines shaped like torpedoes and wings slimmer and meant for combat.

The men in them were young and eager. They had not seen the battle or felt the terrible tensions of aerial combat. They knew only the excitement of the sky, the wild thrill of a roll or the crazy landscape-turning manoeuvre of looping the loop.

It was fun and a magnificent game and they were still mischievous like children with a marvellous toy and like children they got into mischief, barnstorming haystacks and frightening local residents and livestock with some daredevil flying.

This enraged their instructors and their commanding officer, Wing Commander Vines, and particularly their Disciplinary Warrant Officer DWO Wiles, whose moustache bristled at such behaviour. Some were grounded for a time as punishment and some were confined to barracks and given menial tasks under the DWO's fierce and alert eye.

But you had to be careful with spirited young men, for it was their spirit harnessed to their skill that could make them good fliers, and they were needed desperately.

On this morning in 1941 one of them, Leading Aircraftsman and trainee pilot John Grice, was flying solo in his aircraft. He was feeling exhilarated by the rush of the wind past his open cockpit, by the noise of the busy engine, by the feel of the controls in his hands and the fact that he was alone and solely responsible.

He also happened to be the one who gave DWO Wiles, that strutting old walrus, the most trouble.

And John Grice couldn't resist haystacks. He liked to roar over them at a low altitude and make the straw lift on them like hairs on a frightened head.

He saw a haystack below him. He put the nose of his aircraft down and lined up the yellow oblong below.

"Haystack at six o'clock," he shouted, "Tallyho!"

This time it wasn't quite the same. There was someone on the haystack.

The boy on the haystack, twelve-year-old Paul Sims, wasn't feeling particularly energetic in the warm Saturday afternoon. A part of the stack had been opened to get the hay and he drove the shining prongs of the long pitchfork into a sheaf and tossed it down none too expertly to Curtiss Longfer, the sharefarmer who lived in a little lean-to house on their property and helped the boy's widowed mother with the farm.

The sheaf, in fact, hit Curtiss on the head. A hard old head it was without much hair and wearing an old straw hat that fell off. But it wasn't a head that liked being hit by sheaves from a well-built boy who was being sloppy with his work.

"Watch out what you're doing, lad. Keep your mind on your job."

Paul found it hard to keep his mind on anything. The stack smelt of mice. A hopeful hawk hovered about him, waiting. He wondered whether his lively forthright sister, Nancy, was cooking scones for tea or whether Jody, the girl at the next farm, was coming over. A good sensible friend, Jody. Nearly as nice as Nancy, who was a high-spirited teasing kind of sister with a mind of her own who understood him better than even his mother and Curtiss.

Old Curtiss—Gunner Curtiss limping with a wound from the First War. Solid, reliable Curtiss except when he got on the grog once in a while and retired to his little house for a day or so.

"It's what he suffered at the Great War," Nancy told Paul. "We understand. We must help him."

Some people didn't and said nasty things about Curtiss. One was Mrs Marchington Moss, the local grazier's wife who was always wanting to run everyone and everything. An old busybody. They called her "The Duchess".

"What are you doing up there, lad? Daydreaming again?" It was Curtiss. "We got this dray to load and we got chaff to cut. The sheaves won't load themselves."

The boy drove his fork into another sheaf. And then he heard the aeroplane and looked up. It was diving straight at him out of a blue sky.

He could see the wings, the struts, the faint circle of its madly spinning propeller, the wheels, and the black head of the pilot.

He gave a yell and jumped straight off the stack on top of Curtiss. The plane went over with a roar, climbing at the last minute, its slipstream lifting the ends of the sheaves and leaving them jutting like so many upswept beards.

It was too much for old Bessie the horse: the yells and thumps in the dray behind her and then the thing going over, the awful, roaring, windy thing.

She bolted straight out of the stack yard and down the road, the reins trailing uselessly behind her rump and the man and the boy floundering around in the hay.

Straight down the road while the spiteful little plane climbed into the sky, and the hawk, startled for once out of its feathered wits, flew off to somewhere quieter.

The dray rattled and quivered, its iron-rimmed wheels struck stones and potholes and, at every bump, another sheaf fell off.

The boy shook himself free from Curtiss who'd got his foot caught in a hollow in the hay and was desperately trying to free it. Paul saw the reins dragging down around the horse's hoofs and he balanced himself dangerously on the shaft, frantically trying to gather them in. The dray was rocking from side to side and it kept sprinkling sheaves along the road in an untidy line.

Paul picked up one rein but one rein wasn't much good and when he heaved on it the bit in Bessie's frothing mouth made her veer and that didn't do much good either. It headed her for the side of the road and, worse still, for a big strainer post in the fence and even worse than that, for a man sitting against it and wearing, of all things, a tin bowl on his head.

Perce wore the tin bowl as a protection against the magpies which hated him. Perce was an old soldier and had worn tin hats in the war and had a lot of respect for

11

them. They'd kept out the enemy shrapnel on more than one occasion. Perce had been a driver in the Great War and he'd loved horses. War was no place for horses any more than it was a place for men.

Horses screamed like any other wounded. And he decided after the war he'd make it up to them.

So while many farmers had tractors, he stuck to horses just as Curtiss did. And on his farm the animals did as they pleased, particularly Perce's big slow Clydesdales who were active with their jaws among the bran and chaff in the stable but lackadaisical with their shining backsides when hauling Perce's farm implements.

Even his chickens roosted in his car, which had earned it the name of the Chook Chariot, particularly when one evening he'd absentmindedly driven down the township street with a sleepy dazed fowl sitting on the hood.

Even the fencing post he sat against now had white ants which should have been exterminated long ago. But Perce said there was enough extermination going on. So he let things be. He was a local preacher and he preached brotherly love. From morning until night and particularly on Sundays. People laughed at him but they respected him.

And when Curtiss had his bad times at the Sims' farm Perce would go and calm him down. Sitting and talking. Perce knew what made Curtiss act the way he did. He understood. He'd seen the terror and sadness of war. So people respected him. Eccentric, they'd say, but his heart's in the right place. His kitchen table covered with jam tins and the dogs allowed inside. But he'd never do anyone a bad turn.

So he really didn't have enemies. Except the magpies. Although he didn't altogether approve of some of the reckless young devils who flew the aeroplanes.

He'd heard one go over just now, far too low. He shifted his back against the old post. It was a wonder the white ants didn't eat clean through his backbone, people said. But he liked it there. In the sweet air of the paddocks.

Then a sound of hooves, of jingling harness, yells and an awful rattling came up the road and there burst into sight an old sweating horse, a boy balanced on the shafts of the dray it hauled, and frantically grappling with reins, sheaves tossing everywhere and the whole circus headed straight for his post.

The next moments were pandemonium. For Paul there were frightening seconds as the dray went over and the horse with it, the air full of flying sheaves. The sheaves saved him. Their dusty cascade made a straw mattress on which he crashed, the wind going out of him and the dust coming in. For a moment after the frenzy there was complete silence. Then the boy pushed his way out of the hay, a trickle of blood down his nose.

His immediate concern was for Curtiss. But Curtiss must be all right judging by the swearing. And there was Perce, of all people, picking himself up off the ground and using some picturesque Biblical language that included damnation and hell fire.

And there was someone else, a girl, an anxious girl, who had arrived from somewhere on horseback, who was pulling the sheaves from him.

"You all right?"

"Heck Jody, where'd you come from?"

"Down the road. You all right?"

"Yes, I'm OK. Curtiss sounds as if he's OK and we knocked over Perce."

Jody, satisfied about the humans, was now quietening the struggling Bessie, getting the horse back on her feet, making sure there were no serious injuries. Jody Carson loved horses. She had a way with them. She spoke soothingly, running her reassuring strong young hands over the horse's nose as Paul unhitched the traces from the dray. The dray was in a bad way. It had lost a shaft, one wheel was off. The fencing post was in an even worse state. It had collapsed completely, and part of the fence with it, and the ground was covered, it seemed, with homeless termites.

"That's a beaut bruise, Paul and a nice bleeding nose," said Jody. "Better have my handkerchief."

"I'm OK, Jody. Thanks for helping."

"I saw the plane diving at the haystack. Stupid. The pilot can't know anything about horses."

Trust Jody to think of the horse.

Meanwhile the two old warriors were now working themselves into a fine lather.

"Smashed a good dray. That'll be compensation from the Commonwealth. Taxpayers' money will have to pay for this," said Curtiss.

"We'll go back to my place and get the car. And then we'll pay a call on the Air Force," Perce was raising his voice. "I want you all to come as material witnesses."

"Conduct prejudicial to good order and discipline," stormed Curtiss, lapsing into old Army language.

14

"I wouldn't miss it for worlds," said Jody. They pushed the ruined dray against the fence and then the angry procession set off for Perce's house, the two older men in front waving their arms at each other, the girl and boy leading their horses.

Back at his farm, Perce bustled the fowls out of the Chook Chariot on to the verandah, Jody and Paul saw the horses into a yard and gave them a drink. Curtiss stumped up and down like a general marshalling his army.

Then into the car they piled, or rather three of them did. Paul had to crank it while Perce worked the spark and pulled the choke out.

Suddenly the car blurted from its exhaust and gave a treacherous lunge at Paul who quickly sidestepped.

The engine took on an asthmatic cough and rumbled.

Then they were on their way with a terrible grating of gears, Curtiss sitting bolt upright in the front alongside the driver.

"It's war all right," said Jody. "The old soldiers are thirsting for blood. Onward, men. Give no quarter."

She laughed and leant back in the faded old leather seat and fluttered her eyelashes at Paul. Paul laughed. The girl was lively and witty and the boy quieter but there was a nice balance of equality between them.

You're a mischievous girl, he thought, but you're fun, Jody.

2. Crime and Punishment

Jody and Paul knew that the old car wasn't going to stop at the Air Force gate because of the way Perce began working his levers and sparks, grating his gears and blowing his horn.

The sentry knew, too, because he leapt from the path of the car as it went through a wooden boom which cracked and disintegrated. The car surprised a group of drilling airmen who ran in all directions. Perce applied his hand-brake as a last resort but it did no more than surprise a spider that had spun a leisurely web there. He tried to swing the wheel but the accelerator seemed to be jammed and the steering affected by the collision with the barrier.

"Hang on," roared Perce as if everyone wasn't doing it and for dear life. The stubborn car with the gleaming radiator mascot of an Indian's head was on the warpath. It didn't stop until it had buried its bonnet with a terrible crash in the tin and wood wall of a building, sending the car's occupants rolling and colliding with each other, more alarmed than hurt.

"Struth," said Perce, his fears dividing themselves between the state of his car and the condition of its occupants.

"Everyone all right?" he cried. They seemed to be,

shaking bruised limbs and straightening themselves. Perce was meanwhile peering at a notice board that had come skidding over to the radiator to rest against the cracked windscreen. He read the letters on the notice: STATION HEADQUARTERS.

"Struth," he said and this time more slowly.

Wing Commander Vines was wondering how it could all happen so quickly and why it should happen to him. . . .

One moment sitting peacefully enough at his disciplined desk, occupied with all the paperwork and pondering and decision-making of a commanding officer at an Air Force station training young, keen and often reckless men to fly, and the next, seeing the neat wall opposite with its charts and maps bulge inwards with a steaming radiator and an Indian's head poking through.

One moment enjoying the curt, to-the-point but helpful remarks of Disciplinary Warrant Officer Wiles who had been invited to a morning cup of tea, DWO Wiles with an immaculate uniform and immaculate service manners and, next moment, DWO Wiles sitting on the floor covered with tea, with random drops dripping from his beautifully groomed moustache.

Well it had happened and everything for a moment was pandemonium, officers and men running, the fire tender whooping across the parade ground, followed by the stand-by ambulance and followed by just about everyone on the station.

Out of the car had crawled, with help from the growing group of airmen, a big man whose only conversation consisted of the word "Struth", a shorter, shaken, more irascible man who was very conversational indeed and a girl and a boy each about twelve, the boy with bruised forehead and a bleeding nose and the girl with a lively interest in everything that was going on.

"Anyone hurt?" asked Wing Commander Vines, taking charge. The newly arrived quartet of civilians surveyed him with varying degrees of hostility and interest.

"Me car's had a nasty knock. Curtiss ain't hurt, in the tongue anyway. The boy and girl seem all right, more's the wonder. And me name's Perce Pullner."

"Then I'll ask you, Mr Pullner," roared the CO, "what the hell do you mean by driving slapbang into my headquarters?"

"And I'll ask you," Perce roared back, forgetting brotherly love, "what do you mean by letting your airman dive slapbang at a haystack, sending a horse bolting down the road, putting life and limb of three people at risk, and smashing a good dray. Where's your discipline, mister?"

"Discipline," interrupted Curtiss. "This ain't the Army, Perce. This is a mob of school boys in pretty uniforms. Blue orchids, that's what they all are."

The CO flushed at the mention of the blue, for his uniform was an immaculate blue as it happened. And he was well aware of the Air Force's disrespectful nickname.

"Heavens," said Jody in a low voice to Paul, "war's going to start at any moment."

The remarks stung the CO into raising his voice even further. This was his office after all, his station and his service. He didn't usually raise his voice. He left that to people like DWOs who had big voices in constant training. But he raised it now. Besides, the old car's radiator was leaking on his floor and its Indian chief mascot was staring at him with dumb insolence.

"DWO Wiles," he shouted, "where's the chief instructor? I want to know who was flying this morning and who's responsible for this and I want to know *immediately*."

But a calmer air was prevailing. Airmen began extricating the car. A medical orderly had a look at Paul's forehead, dabbed it with antiseptic and put some plaster on it.

"Just a bump, lad," he said. "You'll be all right."

Chairs were brought, cups of tea rushed in by watchful orderlies. Everyone knew it was a crisis.

"Please be seated, everyone," the CO's voice had a more moderate tone. "You all right, lad?" to Paul. "And what about you, miss?"

"I'm all right too," she said. She was still a bit shaken but too interested in the activity and confrontation to worry much about the shock.

"Perhaps one of you would like to tell me about it," Wing Commander Vines said.

He nodded at a hovering orderly. "Corporal, make a note of this, will you?"

Paul was the first. After all it had begun with him on the haystack.

"How low was the plane, lad?"

"I didn't stop to see. I thought it would bounce off the stack."

"I see."

"It stood the sheaves up like tussocks," interrupted

19

Curtiss and then went on with his part of the story.

Perce pounded the table about his strainer post.

"You often sit against a post on the road?" the CO asked. It seemed a bit unusual to him.

"Only when I'm thinking," said Perce. "If a man can't lean against his own post! This is a free country."

"We're trying to keep it that way," the CO said.

"And you, miss. When did you come into it?"

Jody had her head on one side and the CO smiled at her. He had a daughter like that. He wondered what she was doing.

"I came along on my horse. Paul was under the sheaves. Curtiss too. Perce was rolling around and I got the horse to its feet."

"Sensible girl," he said.

Then they all stopped. Commands, staccato and rising in intensity, were coming across the parade ground.

"Left right, *left right*" and then the syllables began to run into each other "lefrilefrilefri".

The whole room rattled with it as in came marching a young airman still in flying suit and looking already discomfited with DWO Wiles roaring in his right ear like half a dozen aero engines.

"*Halt.* Stand at attenshun."

"Sir, this is LAC John Grice. The haystack divebomber, sir."

John Grice was tall, fair and had a face that smiled easily. He wasn't smiling now. He kept his eyes straight ahead, his thumbs at the seam, his back like a ramrod, but he'd seen enough as he'd marched in to know he was for it.

Wiles roaring like a hurricane, the CO actually going red, two older angry-looking civilians, a boy with a patch of sticking plaster and a girl who seemed the most relaxed of all.

"Was it you, Grice?" The CO was even more angry. This was his best potential pilot and also his worst troublemaker.

"Yes, sir."

"You've damaged civilian property, put an aircraft at risk, could have caused serious injury *and disobeyed standing orders*."

"Sir."

They were all watching him.

"You could be grounded for this. Kicked out of flying."

That hurt. The girl noticed the young man's sudden look of pain and contrition.

"There'll be compensation for the dray and we'll fix your car, Mr Pullner," the CO said. "We'll probably fix the dray too. Our riggers and mechanics are pretty versatile."

"That leaves us with LAC Grice," he said looking around. He thought he detected a slight lessening of hostility. The girl was certainly interested, the boy who had been so careful and clear with his explanations leant forward slightly, the two old fire-eaters were into their second cup of tea.

"You men at the First War?" the CO asked. They looked as if they might have been. They nodded: "With the AIF."

"Then you know how these things happen. High spirits.

Everyone wants to be a daredevil. It's no easy job we're sending them to. After all, it's war."

It's war after all, thought Curtiss, and paused, his cup halfway to his mouth, and remembering.

"We know what it's about," said Perce aloud, thinking back.

"You can bring a civil charge if you wish."

"Well, if the vehicles are being repaired..." began Perce.

"You, Grice, I'll attend to later. You're grounded and confined to barracks. March him off, WO."

"About my flying, sir..." began Grice.

"Attention and no talking. About turn, quick *march* lefrilefrilefri." Away went DWO Wiles barking like a great watchdog.

"Will he be grounded?" This came from Paul.

"He'll be charged and his record examined."

"If he had a civilian punishment as well would that help?"

"It might. What's on your mind, er..." asked the CO watching the boy closely.

"Paul," said Jody. "His name's Paul, mine's Jody. Put that down, corporal," she said to the corporal still hovering with the notebook.

Paul couldn't quite explain it. It had come in a flash, amid the sound of little aeroplanes landing and taking off outside, and noticing the look in LAC Grice's eyes at the thought of not flying. Paul was sensible and concerned about the important things, a bit rackety sometimes, but he tried to think things through and look beyond what was

22

happening now and try to imagine what might happen later. Jody always called it fusspotting but she respected him for it. He didn't fly off the handle like some people did but hung on to it and gave it a few turns to see what would happen. When he did fly off, it was look out!

The CO stepped in: "If there was some kind of civilian punishment, I mean, outside the law that is. Perhaps good works, helping the civilian war effort, it might be a mitigating circumstance."

Paul thought about it. This could hardly be called assisting the war effort although it was work of a sort.

"You're the injured party, Paul," said the CO. "You suggest something. And we'll consider it."

So he made his suggestion.. The CO whistled, Curtiss frowned because he thought he saw a motive behind it. What some people called an ulterior motive.

"Bravo," said Jody.

"It seems an unusual but not unfair solution," said the CO. "Now we'll get someone to ring everyone's home and say you're all safe. Then how about some lunch?"

Everyone was agreeable. Perce saw his old car being towed off by Air Force mechanics and a lorry had been dispatched to pick up the dray.

"That was pretty cunning, Paul," said Jody as they walked to the officers' mess.

He wasn't listening. He was watching a Tiger Moth take off, lifting its tail and then its nose, the blur of its propeller, the glint of its wings. It must be really something to fly.

Really something.

23

3. Miranda Makes a Match

Paul woke early, the sun brilliant through the window, the air full of hay smell.

"Up, up, up!" He felt the bedclothes pulled off him and his sister Nancy was there, Nancy who was twenty, lively, long-legged, fair cascading hair.

"I hear the Air Force is coming today," she said. "And that's not all I hear."

"What else?" he said sleepily. He liked his sister. They shared things—the secrets along the creek, the blue heron that lived there, the brown snake they saw moving away once like a whiplash. She understood him, his sleeping in, the way he had to be kept at his jobs. She also understood his loyalty which was something she liked. He thought Nancy the prettiest girl he'd ever seen. And that included Jody who wasn't bad either. He thought so now.

"I hear that the Air Force was nearly demolished by an old bomb, that Curtiss is limping around on his war-wound leg, that Perce's car is propped up in a hangar and that someone with the wisdom of Solomon and a ton of cheek has suggested jobs for the guilty party on this very farm.

"Now get up, Paul," she said. He slid out of bed, climbed into his clothes. His mother had his breakfast ready in the kitchen. Curtiss was there busy with the toast.

24

"Late again," said Mrs Sims. She was a quiet woman, orderly, worrying about the farm when the seasons were bad, about Curtiss when he got drunk and about her son who at times could be lazy and her daughter who was full of spirits and who was her joy, but who could also be wilful. In her quiet way she kept the family together and let its members know she expected things from them, help and understanding which she usually got.

"Jody's here already," said Nancy, looking out of the window.

"Hi, everyone. Thought I'd come and see the pigsty cleaning," Jody said, prancing through the door.

"Cleaning the pigsty...so that's it," said Nancy. "What a brilliantly cunning idea. Just when it's a fortnight overdue for a clean, when Miranda's at her messiest. Hadn't someone better tell her she's about to have a visit from an airman and a pilot? She'll swoon clean into her slops."

"It's punishment," said Paul.

"Indeed," said Nancy, peering at him. "It's good to know that some people get their deserts. Hey," she said, "they're here already. An officer with a moustache, a driver and a very crestfallen young airman."

They all went out, Paul with egg on his mouth, Jody smiling, Nancy curious and amused, Mrs Sims a little worried about whether it was quite the thing and Curtiss ready to do a bit of supervising.

DWO Wiles gave a splendid salute, his arm bouncing up as if on a spring. "Morning everyone. I'm DWO Wiles. I've met Paul and Jody and Mr Curtiss and you

25

"must be Mrs Sims and this must be . . ."

"Nancy," Nancy said, "Nancy Sims."

"And this crestfallen airman in the fatigues and carrying a service issue shovel is Leading Aircraftsman and trainee pilot John Grice who is on punishment. All right, punishment detail, *Tenshun*. To the pigsty, quick march."

"This way," said Paul and away they all went, Tops the dog barking ahead, DWO Wiles swinging his arm briskly and putting on a show and everyone else following in a straggling line, while an amused driver waited in the jeep.

Trainee pilot John Grice's face fell a thousand miles when he saw the pigsty. Miranda the pig greeted him with an earthquake grunt. She was a huge white pig, that's if you could ever see she was white, although certainly you could see that she was large. It was her sty that caught Grice's eye for Miranda lived a messy, congested life even for a pig. Her life revolved around meal times and an occasional forage in the paddock.

"It can't have been cleaned for a year," said LAC Grice.

"Silence. Fatigue party halt, to the pigsty, *Break off*," said DWO Wiles.

"Here is a pair of rubber boots," said Nancy. "I hope they fit, and I'll bring tea down later."

John Grice was still staring at the sty, at the churned-up, straw-mixed, smelly scene. For a moment they all stared at it.

"Aren't you going to let the pig out while I work?" he said. He didn't fancy Miranda. She was too big and too friendly.

26

"She roots up the paddock and Curtiss doesn't like it."
Paul was determined that the job was to be done properly.
Grice could see that. Paul would insist on maximum effort.
The boy would have no mercy. He would see that every
smelly nook and every filthy cranny was cleaned. John
Grice wished Nancy would supervise. But Nancy was
already going with her mother and DWO Wiles who had
been invited for a morning cuppa and he was alone in the
pigsty with Miranda, while Paul began pointing where he
should start and Jody sat on the rail, rather like a spectator
at a bullfight, although no fastidious toreador would ever
have come within a mile of the place.

So he made a start. He began shovelling the muck over
the rail to a heap there. He was nervous of Miranda. In
her huge fat way she had taken a liking to him. Most humans sooner or later signalled a filled trough of sour milk,
old bread, peel and barley. She took him suddenly by surprise and planted a huge heavy trotter on one of his rubber
boots. John gave a yell and lifted his leg. The boot remained embedded in the mud, held firmly by the sow's
leg. He hopped around the sty on one leg while Jody
nearly fell off the rail laughing.

It was while he was unbalanced that Miranda made a
lunge at him, impatient now that the sour milk hadn't appeared. And over he went. For one moment his face came
in contact with the pig's hairy flank, rough, smelly and
slippery and then he slid with a splash into the odorous
swamp that was the floor of the pigsty.

Miranda grunted in irritation at the prone figure and
moved forward to investigate. John Grice found himself ly-

27

ing there looking at the pig's great jowls a few inches from his nose, jowls with small alert eyes above them, the great fat pink upturned nose pushed enquiringly towards him. And the awful thought came into his mind that he had read somewhere that pigs were cannibals and ate their young. What if this great, grunting hulk turned nasty and started eating him. What an ignominious end. "Here lies LAC Grice eaten by a pig called Miranda. Rest in peace, what's left of him."

"She'll roll on you if you aren't careful," Paul warned him. "Get up and we'll squirt you down with the hose. Jody has it ready."

Grice climbed to his feet and a stream of water hit him. It was reticulated water and had good pressure. It was also icy cold and Jody did a thorough job saturating every inch of his skin and clothing, it seemed.

"Hey," he yelled. "Go easy."

"You haven't finished yet, you've barely started," Paul said. John Grice was right about Paul, a slave driver and a perfectionist when other people were doing the work.

But nevertheless he began pitching into the sty or rather pitching out of it; the heap of muck grew. He worked with a will for he was feeling chilly, he longed for clean warm clothes, for a flying suit and the breezy cockpit of his training plane.

"I bet you wish you were flying," said Jody, reading his mind.

"I bet I wish I was," he said.

"If you hadn't been shooting up our haystack you wouldn't be here. You have to get inside that little shed and clean out the straw too,'' said Paul relentlessly.

When Nancy brought the morning lunch she hardly recognised the grubby, saturated figure in the sty. When his face turned toward her she knew it was the lately daring young man of the Tiger Moth.

"He's got himself in a mess. He slipped over," said Paul.

"And we hosed him," said Jody. "We'll hose him again before he sits down to lunch."

LAC Grice didn't wait for the hose. He leapt out of the sty, dried himself on a handy bit of bag, and declared himself ready for lunch. Nancy poured the tea, laid out two plates which contained sandwiches and scones and sat back looking at the pig cleaner.

"Your brother is as bad as our Disciplinary Warrant Officer Wiles," he said. "It's like rowing on a Roman galley. You sure you haven't got any whips around he'll use on me?"

Miranda grunted furiously, still hopeful.

"And that pig in there. She's as big as a tank and as dangerous."

"We breed from her," said Nancy. "She really has a very good pedigree."

John Grice took a long swig of tea. "Ah, that's marvellous. You the tea maker, Nancy?"

"Yes," she said.

"That's why it's so sweet then."

The girls seemed to enjoy the remark. Paul scowled slightly.

"You like flying?" It was the younger girl, Jody.

"There's nothing better. Up there in the sky like a bird. Especially when you're flying solo."

"Birds don't have engines," Paul said.

"My brother," said Nancy, "is a stickler for facts. You may have noticed."

"I've noticed that he's a stickler for pigsty cleaning," said John. He liked Nancy, he liked her more every minute and he kept looking at her. She didn't seem to mind although he noticed her brother did, for Paul was positively glaring.

"You ever been in a plane, Nancy?"

"Heavens no, just watched them fly over."

"It's the sense of being alone, being your own man, the freedom," he said, looking up at the sky. "You're closer to the stars up there."

"You sound like a romantic," said Nancy and then more seriously, "But it's war too, isn't it? In the end. In the end you go up to fight."

"Yes," he said slowly. "We're needed badly. Not that I'm a hero," he added quickly. "And I like flying for itself."

They were all quiet for a moment. Miranda grunted in her sty; she hadn't given up hope for a meal. Miranda never lost hope.

"I want to fly fighters," John Grice said, "I like to be my own man."

"Well now you've finished, you'd better come up to the house and dry yourself properly. He's finished, hasn't he, Paul?"

"There's some old straw left in the sty . . ." Paul began.

30

"Oh come off it, Paul," Nancy laughed. "The sty hasn't been so clean for years. You coming, Jody?"

"I'll stay with Paul," said Jody. She thought Paul looked displeased standing watching Nancy and John walk away. Nancy was laughing and John was waving his hands in a swooping motion and probably he was talking aeroplanes. Paul still scowled, deciding it was conduct unbecoming to a pigsty cleaner.

"Don't be too hard on him, Paul," said Jody, watching him in her shrewd way. "He's going off to fight, isn't he?"

Jody saw more than the boy had seen. She was wise in her way and felt for people. She saw something in John Grice's eyes that wasn't all fun when the war was mentioned.

"You're a stupid old pig," Paul said suddenly to Miranda as he filled her trough. Miranda didn't answer. Her great snout was already buried in her food and her ridiculous tail quivered with enjoyment.

4. The Beckoning Sky

Nancy went out dancing and to the pictures with John when his "sentence" at the station was lifted. In fact she always seemed to be going out with him.

Paul was annoyed but Jody said: "They like each other, can't you see?"

Sometimes she thought Paul was stupid. For she could see it all very plainly.

"You're going out with John a lot," Paul said to Nancy, seeing her preparing to go out on one more Saturday evening.

"You're jealous, I'd say," she said. She looked happy, happier than she had for ages.

"You're not getting too involved, Nancy?" Mrs Sims worried in the background. "He'll be going away soon. Don't put too much store by it. Don't get hurt."

"I'll look after myself, mother," Nancy said. There was a rebellious lift to her chin. But Sunday night John was there for tea and Curtiss joined them, saying in a surprisingly pompous way for him, "Of course this war's not like the last one."

And then he contradicted himself by saying, "There's nothing good you can say about any war."

And looked solemn and had a second cup of tea.

But John Grice brought an excitement to the house that it had never experienced before. He brought flowers for Nancy's mother, calling her Mum and shamelessly wooing her, doing the washing up with Nancy (which Paul didn't mind because he usually did it). Paul told himself that he wasn't jealous of all the attention John Grice paid to Nancy but he couldn't help feeling a twinge. He certainly hadn't felt it before when young men paid attention to his sister and several had, and not with any great success in spite of their new cars and new horses and boxes of chocolates (one box must have been in the shop since the last heatwave, judging by the strange colours of the chocolates inside). But John Grice knew how to make friends.

He called Curtiss "General" because Curtiss was now a sergeant in the Volunteer Defence Corps, a group of older men who drilled on Saturdays and had a variety of uniforms and old guns. Curtiss had been a bit reluctant to talk about them, particularly after their efforts one morning at the bombing range. One clumsy fellow had flung a grenade straight into the air instead of out into the range and everyone scrambled from the trench for their lives, running and flinging themselves flat. Fortunately it hadn't exploded. In fact it had been found to be harmless with the charge withdrawn. Curtiss reported the incident one evening when they were all at tea and when they'd all finished laughing Paul's mother said seriously the men were doing their best.

Curtiss said that the most dangerous enemy the members of the VDC were ever likely to meet was themselves.

"At least they don't shoot up haystacks," said Nancy, with a glance at John.

"Hey, let's have a flying lesson," he said suddenly. He brought a broomstick, sat in a chair and said, "Now this is the joystick. Don't clutch it, handle it gently. This is the way we bank. Now a turn. This footstool's the rudder bar."

The enthusiasm burst out of him like a wave. Nancy took a turn in the chair with the broomstick and then Paul did and imagined himself in the sky in a windy, noisy plane.

"Well," said John, "I might be able to get you a flip, Paul. I could pull a few strings. With DWO Wiles perhaps. He seems to like this family. Come to think of it, I seem to like this family."

He smiled at Nancy and she smiled back and Mrs Sims looked at them both in her quiet, concerned way and Curtiss went on drinking his tea.

"Hey, you mean it about the flight? I could really go up in one of the Tiger Moths?" Paul suddenly burst out. "Up there. That'd be great."

He began to see John Grice in a slightly different way. They all noticed it and laughed.

"Whoa now," Nancy said. "He said he *might* be able to."

"I'll look into it," said John.

"I'd be nervous about it," said Mrs Sims. "I'd have to think about it."

"Mum, I'd have someone flying me," Paul said in his eagerness.

34

"Hark at Kingsford Smith," said Nancy, then she looked at the clock.

"News time," she said, switching on the radio. Big Ben boomed away in London on the news relay and then war came back again into the bright room, into the fun, the girl's expression changing from lightheartedness, the young man's becoming thoughtful. Bombs on London, retreats in the desert. The war was there.

"Well," said John Grice, "back to the Air Force on my stouthearted motorbike."

Nancy went to see him off and they talked at the gate. Curtiss still smoked solemnly on his old pipe, watching its glowing bowl as if it were some tiny screen on which he saw many things.

"Done your chores?" Mrs Sims asked Paul.

A moment later the motorbike sound kicked away into the night until it was gone and the wind drowsed through the pepper tree outside the door and Nancy quietly returned.

The next day Paul came home from school and knew there had been an upset. His mother looked pale and Nancy had her head held high and straight. It was so unusual for mother and daughter to quarrel that Paul didn't know what to make of it.

So he stood, listening.

"I'm old enough to know my own mind, mother," she said. "It's just for a weekend. Time's so precious. I'm twenty. I'm not a child."

"A weekend where?" said Paul.

"Just a weekend away."

35

Later John Grice called for her in an old car he had borrowed from somewhere. She kissed her mother and said: "Sorry I was angry. Please don't worry."

She gave Paul a hug and said, "Don't be jealous."

"Hey," said John, "I've arranged for you to go for a flight, Paul, a short one with instructor Flight Lieutenant Inster if your mother gives her permission—in writing of course." He mocked the straitlaced language of the Air Force.

"Isn't that wonderful, Paul," said Nancy as she climbed into the car. "What you've wanted. You'll have yourself a whale of a time. Why, even I haven't been asked. Just you. Now how's that? Doesn't it take your breath away? You must let him go, Mum. They'd be careful with him."

She looked at her mother again and said: "And don't worry."

Off went the car and Paul stood with his mother, watching it down the lane, the waving figures in it.

"You are worried, Mum," he said quickly.

She looked at him and gave a small smile. "We have to make our own lives, Paul. Time's precious for young people. As Nancy says. So precious."

He thought a moment and then tried it. "Can I go up in the plane? Can I?"

It happened the next day.

DWO Wiles had arrived with an indemnity form just in time for morning tea and a chat with Curtiss. Paul's mother had signed it a little anxiously. And he was off to the Air Force station to fly like a bird, to be a hawk.

Jody pretended to pout. "Ah me, it's a man's world.

36

The poor girls aren't invited. But our time will come."

"Women can't fly," he said.

"Can't they," shouted Jody. "What about Amy Johnson and Jean Batten and Amelia Earhart?"

"Never heard of them."

"Our time will come," she said, a glint in her blue eyes. "Men and boys get tipped out of carts. One day women will take charge and we won't have any more wars. One day I could be Prime Minister."

"What about me?"

"You might get a job cleaning pigsties!" Jody had said.

But now he was at the Air Force station, being fitted out with a helmet too big for his head and goggles which DWO Wiles adjusted. There was a parachute and they fitted his harness. Fortunately he was tall for his years. The CO even came and walked around seeing that the gear was right and a fussy sergeant explained how to pull the ripcord and made him repeat everything.

Flight Lieutenant Inster looked nearly as young as John Grice. He had fair hair and his face was already weatherbeaten and tanned.

"Only a short flight, chum," he said. "No aerobatics. Just a flight as a gesture to the civilian morale."

He gave Paul a long slow wink.

"Well let's be off to the aircraft."

But before Paul went DWO Wiles, who thought of everything, handed him a paper bag, "In case you're sick," he said. "Even tough young fliers have been as sick as dogs."

A few minutes later the little plane was taxying across

the grassy drome, then its engine settled into a roar, it lifted its tail and its nose and it was airborne.

Paul felt the plane lift beneath him, the wind beating back in his face; he saw the blurred circle of the propeller in front of him. He could barely see over the side of the cockpit but he could see enough, the ground inclining steadily away, fences falling back into lines of toy posts, a nearby telephone line marching over a rise with poles looking like matchsticks, houses in miniature, haystacks so tiny he felt he could hold them in his hand. He looked over his shoulder and Flight Lieutenant Inster gave him a grin and a thumbs-up sign and he grinned and gave him one back. Paul's helmet was too big and his goggles were a little loose but he didn't mind.

The feeling he'd had in the pit of his stomach had receded now like the ground.

The land dropped away further and he was conscious of the line of the horizon, hills that slanted as the plane banked slightly. The sea was nearby and the bays and headlands were laid out like models in a geography lesson and the sea had a sheen on it as if it was an enormous piece of silver caught between the darker land.

This was the world of the hawks and the pigeons, of the clouds and the airmen. He didn't know it was so big or that the land was so flat. No wonder John Grice liked it. No wonder the young men became excited in this marvellous, moving, windy, manoeuvrable seat in the sky. No wonder you were closer to the stars and he wondered how it must be at night, under the brilliant planets and the luminous Milky Way.

"Like to handle her a bit?" the voice came through the intercom, a kind of voice pipe, primitive but effective.

"Yes," he said.

"Don't grab the joystick. Don't clutch. Just hold it nice and firm. I'll tell you what to do. I'm here, remember."

Paul did as he was told—push forward and the nose drops, pull back and the nose rises. He worked the rudder bars too, felt the plane change direction, felt it responding, felt it living and throbbing in his hands. He knew the instructor was behind him watching, duplicating, checking. But the boy had an enormous feeling of rapture in the great pavilion of the sky with its curtain of light cloud and its limitless, beckoning space. He was like the hawk. He felt he could fly forever, to the rim of the world, to the stars beyond, to anywhere.

It all ended very quickly. The plane dipped into an air pocket. The wings wobbled and the nose dropped. Paul's stomach dropped with it.

"OK, I've got her. Just a bump in the road," said Flight Lieutenant Inster. "Nothing to worry about."

Paul was past worrying; he had his head down being sick in DWO Wiles's emergency paper bag.

He soon got over it when they landed.

"A bit squeamish? Well it happens to us all," said Flight Lieutenant Inster.

"It was..." the boy paused, lost for words, looking away to the sky over the trees. Looking away, and for a moment, speechless.

The young Flight Lieutenant watched him. He's only a kid, he thought, but he's been bitten by the flying bug. Up there it waits for you. Up there with all the bumps and pockets and updraughts. Up there with a cockpit of dreams that you're the best flier in the world.

What a pity we just can't all fly and be happy. Instead of going up there to kill someone . . . someone who just might like to be happy in a cockpit too.

"Better see that you get home," he said. A jeep drove up with an airman.

The airman saluted, "I have to take the boy home, sir."

Paul shook hands with Flight Lieutenant Inster.

"I did enjoy it," he said. "I know I was sick, but I did enjoy it."

"I know, boy, I enjoyed it too. I always enjoy it," said Flight Lieutenant Inster and watched as the jeep drove Paul away.

He gave his plane a slap of affection.

"Back to work, old girl," he said. "Back to teaching the daring young men."

5. Stand-off in the Store

Paul still couldn't believe he'd flown even if he had been sick. He rushed into the house to tell his mother but she was on the phone to someone, her voice raised, something that was rare. She came away from the phone, looking flushed and angry.

He told her about the flight and she said, "That's nice," but·seemed preoccupied.

When Nancy came home next day Paul rushed out to tell her.

"I've flown," he shouted. "I've flown."

Nancy gave him a hug and kissed her mother warmly.

"We went to the seaside. It was fun," she said. She went to her room to change her clothes.

She came back and they sat down for the meal.

Paul noticed Nancy had a faraway look. She didn't answer when he asked if she'd like the tomato sauce. Her tea remained untouched.

Then she said: "I saw Mrs Marchington Moss, the old busybody, at the beach."

"I know," her mother said. "She rang me about it. She's an overbearing and interfering woman. I won't have insinuations about my daughter."

The girl's colour came up. "How dare she."

It was a bit beyond Paul. Nancy hadn't even asked him any more about his flight and he was bursting to tell her.

Paul didn't realise what gossiping was until he heard Mrs Marchington Moss carrying on about Nancy and John.

And in the local store of all places and before Mrs Nesbit, the size of whose ears was only equalled by that of her tongue. He couldn't believe his ears. What he heard with them.

"This girl Nancy. I saw her with this airman. I was down visiting my sister last weekend at the Bay. Coming out of a hotel they were."

Mrs Nesbit, who could talk and climb shelves, add up grocery lists all at once, nodded and made little clucking noises with her tongue.

"No restraint. Now how about some flour. The war's an excuse ... no restraint at all. And will you have some bacon? It might have been perfectly innocent."

Mrs Marchington Moss had a basket which, like her, was large. Neither of the women noticed Paul behind the broom stand for the store had a variety of goods, most things in fact that country people needed. And gossip, which some customers seemed to need most of all.

"And half a dozen eggs," said Mrs Moss. "My boy is training to join the Air Force and I'm sure he'll know how to behave. Upbringing is so important."

You old turkey, thought the boy. He felt his forehead becoming hot and it was about this time that Nancy would usually touch his arm and say, "Now, Tiger, watch it." Or Jody who could also read the signs would smile and say, "Steady it, scotty breeches." But neither of them was there.

Just the two women talking.

"Some butter, Mrs Moss?"

"With my own eyes I saw them. The mother's a nice woman, but not firm enough. Then there's that head-strong boy and that sharefarmer, what's his name— Curtiss—drinks, I hear."

You've nearly said enough, you old bag, the angry boy thought.

And now bringing poor old Curtiss into it.

"Some tapioca, Mrs Moss? Nice for puddings."

"We can't all just use the war as an excuse and throw off all restraint, and I can tell you, I rang her mother."

"Well I suppose we shouldn't judge."

"These girls. Think they can do what they like. Leading the boys on. They get caught in the end, the hussies . . . and this one is such a miss, this Nancy."

She broke off in surprise. Suddenly confronting her was an angry boy waving a broom. Mrs Moss backed against the counter, shrank against it in fact, which was a feat in itself because she was a big woman and rarely shrank from anything. But she didn't relish the idea of the broom's stiff bristles waving a few inches from her nose.

"Here, Paul," cried Mrs Nesbit. "What are you doing?"

"Don't you talk about my sister and don't you talk about my mother."

Mrs Moss was now leaning backwards over the counter, her face going the colour of the salmon labels. The broom was moving and waving too quickly for her to grab, so Mrs Nesbit came to her aid, out around the counter brandishing a mop handle and for a moment it looked like a deadly duel—boy versus shopkeeper, mop against broom.

"Old gossips. Windbags. You leave my family alone." The boy was beside himself.

"Paul, how dare you!"

"Ring his mother, the little ruffian."

"Get behind me, Mrs Moss." A kettle rattled over and a whole pile of tins crashed as Paul swished the broom menacingly.

He had flown off the handle completely. He was ready to give Mrs Moss a good whack, although Mrs Nesbit was still dancing in front of her ready for battle. Instead he threw the broom with a terrible crash into the hardware section and went stamping out of the shop, forgetting the list he'd brought, his manners and leaving gasps of "Young savage" and "Well I never" and "Didn't I tell you" and "I'll ring his mother."

He wasn't going to put up with these old gossips going on about Nancy or about his mother or even about Curtiss. But particularly about Nancy.

Mrs Marchington Moss had been young once, he supposed. But he bet it was a long time ago. Maybe a hundred years.

He stared at her car. Like her it was big and showy and he bet she sneaked extra petrol from somewhere. He went up and gave the tyres of the car a hard kick. Then he thought of something. He was feeling angry and when he was angry he was likely to do things and then be sorry he'd done them. He stared at the tyres thoughtfully.

Mrs Marchington Moss finally emerged from the shop escorted by Mrs Nesbit like an ocean liner being escorted by a fussing tug. Mrs Nesbit still had the mop handle but the enemy seemed nowhere in sight.

"Needs the discipline of a father. And let me tell you that girl will get herself into a fix if she's not careful. That's if she hasn't already."

"I'll get the rest of the groceries. Oh goodness," suddenly squawked Mrs Nesbit and they both stared at the tyres.

Perce was driving the Chook Chariot into town for a few groceries. The car ran sweetly since the expert fingers of the Air Force mechanics had adjusted its shaky parts. Even the fowls seemed pleased about it and Perce had absent-mindedly shooed a Black Orpington out of the car before he left.

She'd been sitting in the passenger seat but he'd given her a lift with his hand and she'd fluttered off with a loud cackle.

Now he suddenly applied the brakes of the Chook Chariot and thank goodness they were working, for the large irate figure of Mrs Marchington Moss loomed up in the middle of the road, her hands waving like windmills.

He also thought he saw Paul out of the corner of his eye and he wondered whether the boy was up to something.

He wasn't left long in doubt. Mrs Marchington Moss erupted like a volcano.

"Look here, Mr Pullner. You're a friend of that

wretched boy Paul Sims, aren't you? Well, I've just found all my tyres let down. And after he'd behaved like a young savage in the shop, shouting terrible things at us. I thought I was going to be attacked.''

The idea of anybody attacking Mrs Moss seemed pretty remote, Perce thought, but certainly the tyres were flat. He knew Paul didn't do things without a reason, but he didn't enquire what the reason was. Not at the moment.

"Sorry I ain't got a pump, Mrs M. Hop in and I'll drive you to the garage.''

He opened the door and, as she settled suddenly and heavily into the car, he saw something and too late he shouted a warning. A strange expression came over Mrs Moss's face—puzzlement, disbelief and then a kind of anguish.

She leapt from the car with a shriek, Perce's apologies stammering after her. On the back of her dress was a great yellow splotch and a broken shell.

Paul saw it and then grabbed his bicycle and rode home in good spirits.

It had been worth it all to see Mrs Marchington Moss lay an egg.

He came home quietly, put his bike in the shed and went to see his pigeon. He knew that he hadn't done the shopping, that the list remained unticked in his pocket and that the telephone was likely to ring any moment and that retribution was at hand. That was an expression of Perce's he used when preaching and Paul knew retribution was pretty serious and it followed people around who'd been up to mischief. He couldn't see any sign of it at the moment, just his pigeon sitting in its box.

He took the bird down and held it in his hand, felt its warmth and friendliness. Its feathers ruffled a little in the breeze and its head turned quickly this way and that but it was content in his hands; it was used to him. He held it up to his face and the feathers were smooth and the small beak was cool and hard and once it pecked him in an affectionate sort of way.

"Hey," he said, "don't eat me. Eat your wheat."

It made him wonder why pigeons seemed to understand things and people didn't. He liked the bird and liked being with it. He liked watching its soaring, swinging flight. He liked it sitting in his hands.

Birds were like people, he thought, they liked a home and a friend to sit with.

"Hullo, talking to a friend are you?"

It was Nancy who had walked up very quietly.

"Just spending a bit of time with my pigeon."

"Well it's nice to know you have one friend," Nancy said. "You haven't got too many in Yannan at the moment. The telephone's practically rung itself off the pedestal. Mrs Nesbit, then Mrs Marchington Moss, no groceries brought home, and not a brother in sight until now," Nancy said. "Would you like to tell me about it? Or will you come up and tell us all together?"

He climbed up to put the bird back carefully in its box. It made little ducking motions. It began to coo in a low, harmonious way as if it knew he needed soothing.

47

He looked down at the upturned, serious face of his big sister.

"I know you don't behave like that without a reason, Tiger. So out with it. What made you do it?"

She'd guessed but she waited for him to tell her.

"They were saying things."

"About me and John? About the weekend?"

"Yes," he said. "And about Mum too and Curtiss. About everything."

"I thought so," she said. "And it's good that you stick up for everyone. Still, better come and see Mum. She's had Mrs Marchington Moss on the phone for twenty minutes."

Paul made a face. Only one thing was worse than Mrs Marchington Moss in person—it was Mrs Marchington Moss on the other end of a telephone.

6. Fly-past and Farewell

Paul was stacking sheaves on the hay trolly, laying them carefully so the load was neat. The sheaves were arriving regularly on Curtiss's pitchfork from the stooks of hay, little wigwams of sheaves standing in their orderly encampments across the paddock.

The work was also something in the way of punishment for his behaviour in the store. It was hard work even though it was a small load. Curtiss could pitch sheaves with accuracy and fast too and Paul found it difficult keeping up.

He was glad to see Nancy coming across the paddock with the lunch.

"Hullo Tiger," she shouted at him. "Come and have your lunch. Meat pie with one of my best crusts. Hot scones, with running butter. Billy tea. My, how I spoil you both."

Curtiss laid several sheaves as seats in the shadow of the waggon and cut the string of another sheaf so that the horses had something to munch while the people ate. A mouse disturbed ran off but the watchful shadow came out of the sky in a tumbling flash. The hawk flew off for its own lunch on a nearby post.

"Well, what's news, Nancy?" Curtiss asked. He

seemed pleased about the pie and he sat down while Nancy served it on enamel plates, handed round the knives and forks, for lunch in the paddock had its own etiquette. "How's that young haystack bomber?"

"She's always going out with him. He must be all right," said Paul.

"Jealous," she laughed. And then she looked serious. "He'll be posted any time now. They need pilots urgently and he has advanced training to do, probably overseas."

She hung on the word overseas and looked far away.

"He mightn't go that far, Sis," said Paul. "I'd like some more pie."

They were all quiet a moment. Curtiss ate slowly and watched the girl. She felt his wise eyes on her and she flushed a little.

"It's all part of war," she said. "The going away, the parting."

"I'm afraid it is," said Curtiss.

They were quiet again.

"Hey Nancy, is that apple turnover?" Paul said, peering in the basket.

"You've got eyes like that hawk," she said.

Her little moment of sadness was gone.

"He's not a bad stacker, is he, Curtiss?"

Curtiss ran his eyes over the side of the waggon. "There's a few of them sheaves sticking out."

Paul wiped his lips. Curtiss looked a bit stern at the speed in the apple-turnover eating.

"You'll have indigestion one day," he warned. "Now you might fill the waterbag over at the underground tank.

It'll help you digest the apple pie. Nancy and I'll have a little talk.''

Paul walked slowly with the waterbag; Tops, the dog, running ahead, scared a quiet and wise hare from its squat. The dog and the hare had a friendly run down the paddock but the hare dodged suddenly and disappeared into some nearby stubble and the dog pretended a post was more interesting and saluted it in the way that dogs do.

The boy felt the warm sun on him. There was the insistent sound of aircraft in the distance. He thought about them and about the war and people being hurt and dying. And the pictures he saw on the newsreels of aeroplanes leaving long vapour trails in the sky or falling like leaves blown from some smoking bonfire, fluttering over and over, leaving forlorn wisps in the air.

It was quiet apart from the distant planes. A light heat haze hung over the paddock where the stubble stitched its neat seams.

Paul at last came to the old pump which he primed from a dipper of water standing nearby. It needed to be primed and he clanked the pump handle, pouring the water in the top of the pump, hearing the distant trickle of it meeting the waters of the underground tank. He began to pump furiously, the old pump wheezing asthmatically until suddenly the clean sweet water came from the spout and gushed into the dipper. He filled it and transferred it to the waterbag which at once began to sweat through its canvas sides as the water poured in, cooling its interior by evaporation. A simple and wonderful thing was a waterbag.

Curtiss said good water was a beautiful thing: there'd

been times when he was thirsty, tongue stuck to the roof of his mouth, with stinking water everywhere. In the other war that was. He'd told Paul about it in a rare moment.

"So don't you go wasting water, lad. This is a dry country and water's the sweetest thing it's got."

It was a pity, someone had said, Curtiss didn't put more water with his grog when he had his benders but the boy didn't like people who criticised Curtiss.

At last he filled the bag, being careful to fill the dipper for the next person to prime the pump. He also gave Tops a quick fill in an old dish and the dog lapped gratefully.

Paul felt lethargic in the sun and the iron on the old tumbledown shed nearby gave a crack in the heat and he thought, I'd better watch out for snakes. He walked on, and saw a dead lizard and turned it over with his boot after Tops had sniffed it in an authoritative way.

He wondered about things and people dying. Curtiss said everything lived again in some other way. Curtiss had some queer ideas. Perce was more positive: Perce said you either went up or down, to heaven or the other place. There was no halfway house where you could sit around trying to make up your mind.

Paul didn't like to think about young things dying: young lambs and birds. Perhaps everything did live again in some other way.

"What do you think, Tops?" he said. But Tops was looking for the hare again, tail in the proud curl of a knowing country dog out with his young friend.

Paul thought: old wood rots and old chaff goes bad and smells but when you throw it out it seems to mix with the soil and those big mushrooms come up in it.

Then the dead sheep lie in the paddocks and the crows pick their carcasses then you plough them in and the crops seem to grow thicker where they've lain.

But how is it with us, he wondered. Everyone gets buried in a cemetery. It would be better to be buried in the paddock and they'd plough you in and grow wheat on top of you and that would be more sensible, he thought, out in a wide free paddock instead of with dreary rows of heavy tombstones on top and with mourners and visitors running the gauntlet of the bull-ants that ferociously guarded their holes on the cemetery paths.

He'd spoken to Curtiss about it, about dying and Curtiss had given him a quick look and a short answer: "People die and people are born, lad. Old grass withers and new grass grows."

He'd asked his mother about it and told her what Curtiss had said but she said perhaps Curtiss had seen too much dying at the Great War and that's what made him drunk sometimes.

Mind you, Curtiss never got violent or rough, just stayed in his little lean-to house, sometimes playing an old mouth organ with a melody that went staggering through the air as if it was drunk too—sad and drunk and full of tears.

It made Tops the dog howl. "Wassamatter, old son?" Curtiss would say and pat the dog's head and they'd be sad together.

Next day Curtiss would be his hard-working, meticulous self again.

Suddenly Paul was jerked back to the present. Tops was racing across the field, barking in the important way of a dog on his home ground and with a stranger on it.

Paul saw a tall striding figure in Air Force uniform heading for the waggon from a car on the nearby road. The figure had reached the waggon and there was DWO Wiles. Nancy was reading a letter and Curtiss standing chatting.

Nancy turned to Paul with a quick tight smile. "It's very kind of Mr Wiles. He's come to tell us John's had an emergency posting overseas. He can't get leave."

"Sorry to bring bad news, miss," said DWO Wiles. "It's the Service."

Curtiss said: "Have a cup of tea, still a bit in the billy. It's not hot, but thirst-quenching."

The warrant officer seated himself on a sheaf. Paul could see his sister's tense face. She read the letter again. She was getting herself under control but it had been a shock.

Suddenly she sat up straight and listened. There was a plane circling over their farmhouse. Then the pilot must have seen them. For it headed towards them, low but not too low.

The horses lifted their heads and Paul instinctively ran to them. The others jumped to their feet, DWO Wiles already beginning to sense another breach of discipline. He wouldn't be surprised if a certain leading aircraftsman had persuaded a friend to bring him on a last flight. The plane looked like that of Flight Lieutenant Inster who could be easily persuaded into such a mission, having both a kind heart and a way of getting around authority.

54

He believed that daredevil would have landed if the paddock hadn't been full of stooks.

Nancy was already running, waving her scarf. The plane went past. There were two heads in the cockpit. The flier in front waved frantically. The plane banked and came back again, the figure waving. It was Inster's plane all right, mused DWO Wiles, and there was no doubt who the passenger was.

The girl raced along the paddock waving. Then she stopped, still waving, her whole body leaning towards the plane almost as if she wanted a whirlwind to come from its slipstream and suck her up into the sky after it like a beautiful bird.

Paul suddenly felt she had gone away . . . not just down the paddock but away somewhere that they could not see but she could see clearly.

Somewhere beyond them all.

She stood there and the boy went up to her.

"Sis," he said. "He'll be back."

She put her hand into his and smiled a sad little smile.

Tops, the dog, came up the other side of her and put his muzzle into her hand. Tops was a sympathetic dog and had a way of understanding when people were sad.

7. A Walk by the Creek

The weeks went by and the war became more intense overseas. They heard reports on the radio and saw accounts in the paper, pictures of bombings, of blazing ships sinking. There were fund-raising socials in the church hall, people prepared Comforts Fund parcels, knitted for the troops and there were more farewells. More young men were going. Bert, the baker who called with the still warm bread, said goodbye, the driver of the milk lorry, hefting his last cream and milk cans on to the truck with which he visited the farm said, "See you when the war's over." Nancy gave him a little parcel of socks and a scarf.

Mrs Marchington Moss's son was continuing his training in the Air Force. For king and country she said in her pompous way, but Mrs Sims in her charitable fashion said Mrs Moss was a mother like any mother and must be feeling sad and worried.

There was sadness when someone was wounded or someone was killed and Jody and Paul realised that young Stanton Jones from a nearby farm, because of some gritty battle in the Western Desert, wouldn't come home any more or open the bowling for the local cricket team, the red leather ball lifting from the matting-covered wicket on a warm summer afternoon.

They learnt the names of little North African towns and

they heard about submarines in the Atlantic and mines began to sink ships off the Australian coast.

And John wrote to Nancy about his advanced training "somewhere overseas" and the conversion course to fighters that would follow it when he was sent on, being careful about what he said. And Nancy wrote back telling him the small intimate things, the little happenings that would normally seem inconsequential but which men liked to hear when they were far from home.

She seemed more preoccupied and sometimes she looked pale though everybody tried to cheer her up. Then she'd take hold of herself and be happy and bustling again. She walked a lot by the creek and Paul and Tops went with her for company.

The wind sang in the pepper tree, the weeks drifted like the dust, the countryside remained itself with its hares and its hawks and snakes and its sheep, with the rhythm of the seasons.

One afternoon Paul found Nancy waiting for him when he came home from school. She'd been to the nearby town that day wth her mother. It seemed a routine sort of trip.

But Nancy barely gave him time to have his usual glass of cordial.

His mother had greeted him quietly, "Have a good day, Paul?"

"Yes, Mum."

She looked at Nancy.

"Come on, Tiger," Nancy said. "Let's go for a walk along the creek. I've got something to tell."

He liked that, sharing things, it was like the old times.

He liked walking with his sister. He liked the way she was interested in what he said.

She had a keen eye for a nest in a tree, or a lizard on a post. He showed her an old snake skin withered and yet threatening in the grass. He touched it and wondered about the beautiful deadly thing that had shed it, all muscle and whiplash action, a head faster than an arrow. He wasn't afraid of snakes, just respectful of them. Let them mind their own business and catch mice.

"It's a big one," she said, "a big brownie."

"Gee, they're fast, Nancy. Like lightning. Bill Downer even missed one with his shotgun."

"Has he ever hit anything with that shotgun?"

"He hit his tank once when he was trying to shoot a fox after his fowls, and it spouted water like a watering can."

"Paul?"

"Yes," he said, only half listening. Next he was thinking about showing her the parrots he could hear in the trees. He thought he caught the flash of a rosella's plumage . . . there it was like a feathered rainbow.

"Hey Sis, rosellas!"

"Yes," she said, "they're beautiful. Come here and sit beside me." He sat beside her.

He smiled at her because he thought she was the best looking person he'd ever seen. She had hair that was like gold and that wasn't a silly way to describe it, because it had fire in it, like the rosella. He noticed her neck was longer and more graceful and her chin was prettier than most people's. There was an awful lot of people in the district with no necks. Necks seemed to disappear when

58

people got over forty and chins seemed to take over.

Now she looked serious, a little pale.

"It's about John," she said.

"Has he got his commission? Has he?"

She looked at him in her serious way.

"No, it's more important than that."

He whistled and wondered what it could be.

"I'm going to have his baby, Paul."

He didn't know what to say. His mouth fell open and then closed again.

"People will think it's wrong," she said, "our not being married. Mother knows. I know it will be hard for us, for her and for me. But I want the baby, Paul."

"There's a war on. Things aren't the same in a war. Curtiss said so. People are away from each other," the boy's words came quickly. He wanted her to know he cared about her and didn't care about what other people thought. He couldn't really say what he thought because he felt it so intensely.

"I'll help look after it. Look, I know how. Bennie's got a baby sister. I've been there when he's been washing her. He's good at it. And there's Jody. Hey, there's Jody."

He said eagerly, "Jody will help."

His face was close to hers. She could see the sweat on his freckled nose.

"And people needn't know, Nancy."

"I'll start to bulge."

"Yes, well you'll have to. There are two people. There'll be two..." he was stammering again, "you know, mothers and babies. I saw Mrs Sydney. She was

59

like a great balloon. And old Dinah when she had puppies. She drooped in the centre, Jody said.''

"Aunt Rosa will have to know," she said.

He groaned. Aunt Rosa talked about sin even if you were cheeky. She was an old mumble bag and was always telling his mother what to do and that boy is getting out of hand and I hope you're keeping your eye on that strong-minded daughter or mark my words. He could hear her voice now, in his mind.

"Can I tell Jody?" he asked.

"Yes you can," she said. "She's a nice girl and she's a good friend and she'll be sensible about it."

She clasped her hands and looked away across the creek, past the trees and the paddocks towards the distant Air Force station. For a moment she was away and sad. The boy could see that. He knew they hadn't much money and that it would be an extra burden for his mother and what would Curtiss say when he knew.

They sat there a moment longer. A hawk fluttered far above them and the sky was an enormous dome full of light and space.

He tried another thought.

"Strawberry never had any trouble with her calf. One minute she was chewing her cud and the next moment there's the calf staggering around."

He was trying to get used to the idea.

"It was a nice calf, a little roan calf," he said.

"I don't think I'll have a little roan baby," she said. "But it's way off yet. Months yet." She drew up her knees and rested her chin.

"People are not going to like it," she said again. "There'll be talk. Will you mind?"

"No, I won't and people better not talk to me," he said.

"I've written to John. I did it straight away. Not because I wanted to worry him. But I knew he would want to know," she said it half to herself.

"Would you like to see the rosellas?" he asked. "They're in the trees over there. I just saw one move."

She didn't answer for a moment. She seemed remote, far away, which was unlike her. She was so forthright and quick to respond to any idea or small excitement he might suggest. He expected her to turn her head quickly towards where the brilliant parrots were squabbling in the tree. But she didn't. She looked away somewhere else. And for a moment he felt a little alone, not unwanted but left out. Certainly she'd told him about the baby and he was trying to understand it all, even screwing up his face again in his earnestness the way he always did at the rare times he concentrated. But he felt now that this was going to change things, that the old times might be gone, the sharing of the small but to him important events that other adults didn't altogether understand or couldn't be bothered with, that this might be at an end because Nancy would have the child to think about and it would complicate the easy, happy run of their lives. The war seemed to be doing that anyway, upsetting everyone and taking people away from each other.

So they stood by the creek and he waited, watching her. Suddenly she shook herself.

"What did you say? I'm sorry, I was dreaming."

61

"The rosellas," Paul said. "See them."

"Yes, I see them. Noisy beggars. Let's go home."

He gave the rosellas a baleful look. "Shut your beaks," he said.

And followed his sister.

Nancy was right about people talking. And right too about her getting big, as the months went by.

"Your sister's got a bun in the oven. And she's not married," said Freddie Nilson at school.

Paul flew at him and the next moment they were rolling around the shelter shed in a welter of schoolbags, apples rolling, squashed sandwiches and children shrieking, with the inevitable arrival of the teacher Miss Ginson trying to separate them.

"Paul, Freddie, stop it," she shouted.

Winnie, the tell-tale, stepped forward, ever eager to oblige. "Freddie said Paul's sister's got a bun in the oven and she's not even married."

She drew back sniggering.

"No more of that talk from anyone, do you hear? From *no one*." Miss Ginson went red with rage.

Freddie's nose had the worst of it and was now bleeding under the tap, his head held down by Miss Ginson. The old school tap from the leaking tank had cooled many a playground hothead.

Jody came rushing back. She'd missed the fight because she was checking on her horse. She took one look at Paul's face and another at Freddie's nose and guessed the rest.

That didn't stop the note-passing and sniggering in

class. Jody intercepted one note from Winnie and tore it up. Then she sent a note back: "Keep your window closed tonight. The masked avenger is abroad."

Winnie looked at the note and then looked at Jody. She was scared of Jody and rolled the note nervously into a ball. Jody drew her finger across her throat and Winnie bent her head to her work, pretending she hadn't seen.

Paul told Nancy about the fight.

"It isn't easy, is it Tiger," said Nancy, "for either of us."

"Hurry up, Paul and dress . . ." It was his mother's voice. "Perce will be here in his car any minute and your partner has just arrived."

There was a burst of laughter and Jody's voice, "See your hair's combed. I don't dance with untidy men."

More laughter followed and Paul looked at himself in the mirror, saw fair, reasonably brushed hair shining in the light, with a couple of pieces that stood up at the back like a cockatoo's crest.

It wasn't his idea to go to Mrs Marchington Moss's stupid woolshed dance. He resented going within ten miles of Mrs M.M., particularly after her nastiness about Nancy and she hadn't been any kinder in the following months. If anything she was worse with her "I-told-you-so" and "it-was-just-as-I-thought" attitude which he knew hurt his mother and angered Nancy. But his mother said it was the proper thing to go and to take some supper and Nancy said that anyway people of her shape couldn't go dancing.

She'd smiled at him, but he knew she was hurt about all

the talk although she'd expected it.

And anyway Jody wanted to go and Perce said he'd take them because he was playing his accordion, one of his accomplishments.

People might laugh about Perce but when they were dancing to his music it did all kinds of things to them. Fat ladies danced like fairies and old farmers were as skittish as colts. And people held each other closer and closed their eyes and sighed like film stars at Perce's music.

And the Air Force was coming; the dance was in aid of the Services. Everything was "in aid" of something.

So he had to go because his mother wanted him to but people had better behave. He came out of his room. Jody, who had a bright dress and a bright look, strutted around him on inspection like Disciplinary Warrant Officer Wiles.

At that moment Perce came in "Good evening everybodying" and Tops the dog put his head inside the door. Tops enjoyed a ride in the car and you had to keep your eyes on him.

"Outside, Tops," said Nancy. "Well, you'd all better be off. Here Paul, here's the supper. Behave yourself."

Her face was serious and a little wistful. There was a tune tinkling on the radio and she began to beat time with her head.

She'd received a long and understanding letter from John's parents. It had comforted her but made her thoughtful and concerned at the same time.

"One day you'll be dancing again, Nancy," Paul said.

"Yes," she said. "One day."

They clambered into Perce's old tourer, Jody in front

and Paul in the back. Jody was learning to drive her family's car and she was interested in the strange collection of gear levers, sparks and chokes in Perce's car. In some ways she was a terrible tomboy even when going dancing.

Perce let out the clutch and off they roared through the brisk country night. It was autumn and the air calm and clear, the stars brilliant.

They were some distance down the road when Paul began sniffing. There was a doggy smell in the back, not surprisingly he supposed because Perce's car was a regular Noah's Ark. The Chook Chariot it might be called but it had also carried calves, muscovy ducks and other odd creatures.

Paul put his hand down and got a sudden lick. He peered down on the floor and there leaning hard against a corner, was Tops. For a moment he was going to tell Perce but Perce and Jody were laughing and talking and even, at one stage, singing, and anyhow if a dog wanted to go along for the ride, why not? He could trot home across the paddocks if he got tired of it.

"Have a sausage roll, Tops," he whispered, unearthing one from the basket.

8. The Battering Ram

The woolshed was festooned with streamers and the floor had been prepared with candle grease to make it smooth for dancing and it seemed full of people as they went in, with Air Force officers and men and DWO Wiles with his head shining and his uniform immaculate as usual.

"Where's that car of yours, Perce?" he asked.

"Safely parked," said Perce. His accordion gave a musical wheeze as if it was eager for the fray.

Paul put his basket of food on one of the trestle tables on one side of the room.

"No, not there, boy, not there, that's already set." It was Mrs Marchington Moss, towering and imperious. She snatched it from him.

"It's from my mother and Nancy," he said, hanging on to it until the last minute.

"Is it?" she said. "You behave yourself here tonight, my lad, or look out."

Jody came up quickly because she saw Paul looking angry.

"How are you tonight, Mrs M?" she said brightly.

"My name is Mrs Marchington Moss and not Mrs M. I'm very busy. Here, put those tables over there."

And she was away marshalling people and food, demanding this and directing that, a proper old duchess and a big bag of bossiness, Paul thought.

"You'd better be careful, Paul," Jody said, "or you'll be getting into one of your moods. Be nice. Just for me. You can't change people."

She stood looking at him in her concerned, friendly way and at that moment the master of ceremonies announced the first dance and an old piano, played by some fellow imported from the nearby town, struck up and then Perce's accordion accompanied it.

Perce's music had magic all right, and even Paul felt his not very expert feet beginning to follow its gay old tunes and it seemed to transform Jody. She began to swing and dance, her eyes shone and her hair fell over one eye and her cheeks went red.

Perce played with his head on one side, squeezing and expanding the accordion, rapt in his music. And it filled the shed and went swinging away into the night as if it would set the stars whirling and rock the ascending moon clean out of the sky.

The dance paused for a moment and, as it did, Paul heard two women sitting nearby say, "Yes, that's the boy. It's his sister. It's a wonder she isn't here flaunting herself. Well, it must be a great worry for the mother. No restraint."

No restraint . . . no restraint . . . why were they always saying that?

The music went on again, but Paul didn't dance so happily this time, he wasn't much good at it anyway and he glared at the two women when he went past and, as he wasn't looking where he was going, he ran into Mrs Marchington Moss and a plate of sausage rolls.

"You again," she shouted. "You're a troublemaker. You really are." People were treading sausage rolls into the floor. He went down on his hands and knees to collect them and got his hands trodden on for his trouble.

He rose red-faced as the dance ended and said: "I'm sorry, missus. I didn't see you."

"Really, he didn't," Jody said.

"It would be better if some children stayed at home," said one of the sharp women. "I hear he is a problem too. No restraint in that family."

I'm not a problem, he thought. But I don't care if I am. I don't like the dance and the looks and the talk that's going on.

"You can take a spell," Jody said. "Warrant Officer Wiles has asked me to dance."

"If I may have the honour," said the warrant officer, saluting.

"You can have it if you want to," the boy said, not very graciously.

He went outside while the music went on again. Wooden races led from the side of the shearing shed down into a series of little yards where the sheep were kept for shearing. There were various gates. He saw a little colony of eyes and he suddenly realised that there was a small flock of sheep there probably for crutching—clipping the soiled and matted wool from the sheep's hindquarters—or for some kind of attention in the morning.

There was also another occupant in a pen of his own—a

68

stately ram and Paul knew that this must be Smallacombe Lysander the Second, the great prize ram.

Everyone had heard of Smallacombe Lysander until they were sick of him. Pictures in the papers, a great festoon of prize sashes and cups at the homestead. Wherever sheep breeders gathered, Smallacombe Lysander the Second's name was spoken, if not in whispers then in lowered voices of respect.

The thought of it made Paul even angrier. After all the ram was only a great lump of mutton and his wool probably wouldn't even make a third-rate cardigan.

Paul thought of Nancy at home.

He suddenly saw red or whatever people see when they're angry.

He'd suddenly had an idea. Nobody was there to tell him the idea wasn't going to help anyone. Jody couldn't because she was dancing. DWO Wiles couldn't because he was dancing with Jody. Perce couldn't because he was playing for Jody and DWO Wiles.

And Mrs Marchington Moss, the cause of it all, at that moment decided to raise her voice to its most commanding shout, telling some poor nervous supper preparer to put some cake dish on some table.

And it was the sound of her voice that decided him.

He looked at the sheep again and then he thought, "Tops is a sheep dog."

And Tops was out sitting in the car.

Jody missed Paul after her dance and became worried.

"Has anyone seen Paul?" she asked.

"No we haven't, except when he dropped the sausage

rolls," said a woman crossly. Her scowl vanished to be replaced by one of astonishment.

Jody swung around for a door flew open in the side of the shed and with the yapping of a dog in the distance and a scatter of people, in they came—a small flock of careering, frightened, violently swerving sheep. The dancers screamed, laughed, shouted, dodged and shoved, some trying to steer the sheep into manageable little groups, some falling over each other, the bedlam compounded by a dogfight that suddenly erupted into the hall—dogs, sheep and people, all hopelessly mixed.

Jody's heart sank for she saw a face looking in the door, a face in which guilt, astonishment and glee were all struggling.

"Paul," she gasped, "you did it."

But then there was a dramatic entrance that even stopped a shrieking Mrs Marchington Moss in her outraged tracks. She stood fumbling at her ropes of beads as if wishing she could haul herself up on them and out of danger.

For, blinking angrily and confused in the light and with head lowered, was Smallacombe Lysander the Second.

"Get the ram. Stop the ram. Be careful with the ram," Mrs Marchington Moss began erupting orders that only compounded the confusion.

So men linked their arms and advanced in a human chain towards the ram. But Smallacombe Lysander the Second, normally impeccable before show judges, was as outraged as his mistress. He didn't take kindly to the shoving of his great padded rear and hands trying to steer the

70

arrogant curl of his horns around to a less vulnerable area of the room. He disliked bad handling.

Driven from his quiet pen by a barking dog and a shouting boy, he was in a frenzied state, protesting with a deep baritone bleat. Then came the ultimate protest; he lowered his great battering ram of a head, his eyes glassy with fury. He met Mrs Marchington Moss, his owner who had posed with him a dozen times in the agricultural papers with headlines such as "Woman Grazier Wins Again", "More honours for Lysander"—he met her in front of the trestle table containing the supper centre-pieces of iced cakes, punch bowls and fruit cup.

Mrs Marchington Moss knew that when Lysander put his head down the time for argument was over. With surprising speed for her size, she leaped aside in a flurry of evening dress and a rattle of beads, but not before he had struck her a glancing blow that sent her hissing and wheezing like a punctured football into the arms of DWO Wiles who in turn collapsed into a press of young airmen.

But the central table had taken the full furious impact of the pedigree sheep. The punch and fruit cup exploded in a rainbow geyser towards the roof and then descended in a sweet-tasting shower to spatter screaming women. But it was the last major onslaught of the night. By now most of the sheep had been cornered, the dogfight between Tops and the station dogs had been decided, mainly by Perce separating them with his wheezing, protesting accordion.

People were helping Mrs Marchington Moss to her feet, others were clearing up the mess, men were running for bags and brooms, a group was herding the sheep back to the yards with shouts of "Ho-ho" mingled with baas and bleats. A regular little army surrounded Smallacombe Lysander who left the field of combat with a fine sneer on his long aristocratic face, his great nostrils still blowing pugnacious gusts of air.

And Paul suddenly looked up to see the stern face of DWO Wiles. DWO Wiles had seen the boy after the dramatic entry of the sheep. He knew guilt when he saw it. He had made a study of reading guilty young faces, and he read this one at a glance.

"Conduct prejudicial, lad," said DWO Wiles. Paul knew he was for it.

Jody knew too, feeling angry and sorry and disappointed that the carefree evening was over.

Between them Paul, Tops and Lysander Smallacombe the Second had made a terrible hash of the woolshed-in-aid-of-the-Air-Force dance.

"I can't understand what got into you," Paul's mother said. They all stood in the kitchen. Curtiss was there, smoking a late pipe and shaking his head. Jody was there trying to give Paul support.

Nancy was there in her dressing gown. She knew her brother and she knew he didn't do things for nothing and she half guessed what the cause was. Worst of all, Disciplinary Warrant Officer Wiles was there, representing the Air Force he said.

The only one not present was Tops the dog who, being of a shrewd nature when humans were arguing, had departed to his kennel where he got some comfort from an old bone he always kept to see him through crises.

"Why did you do it, Paul?"

"I didn't like what people were saying."

"They were saying things about me again, weren't they?"

It was Nancy this time.

"I'm not saying," Paul answered.

"He'll be punished," said Mrs Sims. "I'm so ashamed. The ball was in aid of the Air Force and Services."

"May I make a suggestion?" said DWO Wiles.

"Yes," said Mrs Sims.

"The CO would like to see the boy. Tomorrow if possible. It's Saturday. I think there was once a matter of the Air Force being in the wrong and the civilians setting the punishment."

"I seem to remember it," said Curtiss.

"Now we have the situation reversed," said DWO Wiles. "We think it's fair if the boy has a bit of a taste of our discipline. We won't flog him or anything like that. Could he be there in the morning then?"

"Of course he'll be there."

DWO Wiles took his leave.

Paul didn't like the sound of it but he supposed it was fair.

"I'm going too," said Jody. "You'll need a lawyer."

"You're not a lawyer," the boy said.

"Well at least I'm smarter than you are," she said.

He said: "I'll fight my own battles."

She knew that he meant it this time.

73

9. Letters and Lectures

The house was quiet, everyone had gone, his mother in bed and he laid his head on his pillow and wondered what they'd say to him at the Air Force. Wing Commander Vines with three rings on his coat, and DWO Wiles with his handlebar moustache. At least it was safe here in the warm bed with the smooth ironed pillow beneath his head. Outside he could hear Tops scratching a flea, he must have come back again for company. There was one friend anyway and with Jody, maybe two.

Suddenly he saw a light in his sister's room. He was out of bed in a tick and putting his head around her door. "Can't you sleep, Sis?" he said in a low voice.

"No," she said. "The baby's restless. Giving little kicks inside me."

He pattered in. He wanted some sympathy and company too.

"Why are they such kickers, Sis? Why don't they lie quiet and behave themselves until it's time to come out," he said. "They certainly kick and yell then."

"It's life. Life growing," she said. "It's a nice feeling. I'm sorry about all the row. They were talking about me, weren't they? Calling me a shameless hussy or something. I know some of those women. That's what started it all,

74

isn't it? No restraint, I bet that's what they said."

"Yes," he said, "but I don't care."

She gave a little start, "It kicked again."

"It's healthy, isn't it?" He was feeling knowledgeable about babies. He said, "I'll get you some tea. The kettle is on the stove."

"I'd really like a cold drink," she said. "Funny, isn't it. I'd just like some cordial. There's some in the ice chest."

He went to the ice chest and took out the cordial which was already mixed. They got a block of ice on Fridays when Perce picked it up and wrapped it in a bag in his car. He got it at the butter factory. Paul liked visiting the butter factory with the great churns and the huge piston and great flywheel of the steam engine that powered it. The freezing room had blocks of ice piled to the ceiling. It even had icicles and the cold bit into you. It was like being in Antarctica and the ice man wore a bag on his head and looked as if he'd come in from a blizzard somewhere.

Paul took the glass of cordial to Nancy and then sat on the foot of her bed. She could see that he needed company and support. She needed some herself.

"Like to hear my letter from John?"

"It's private, isn't it?"

"Well, some of it is. You know it's daytime in England now."

She paused a moment. The wind, the old steady plains wind, gritty and dry, was singing through the pepper tree outside. The tree made a sad sound. Curtiss had once said its ancestors came from South America, so perhaps it was homesick. Her own mood echoed the lonely, empty sound.

"Are you going to read it, Sis?"

She picked up the letter from the little table beside her bed where a lamp stood and the boy watched her eyes glisten as she opened it and the soft lamplight on her hair and her smooth, serious face.

"The country is beautiful (she read) and with hedgerows and clear streams that run along the fields like water on a green carpet. Different from our dry old country. We don't get much sleep and there aren't very many of us although more are arriving. We seem to be always in the air. Sometimes we are the hawks looking for prey and sometimes we are the prey.

"I think of you and the baby and the coming home. I'm glad my parents have written. Keep the baby safe. How's that other boy, your brother? Behaving himself I hope. I'm sitting in a canvas chair and the sun is shining for once. How's Miranda? I'd even clean her sty just to be near you again, darling. . . ."

"Just to be near you," the girl repeated it and she looked through the window at the night and the clear, far stars above the trees while Paul sat silently. Outside Tops scratched another flea.

Far from the whispering pepper tree and the silent girl and the scratching dog the sky was clear and the weather fine over the patchwork English countryside.

But there was a mêlée of planes over the Channel, one of those sharp encounters of war.

In the frantic little world inside his cockpit John Grice saw the tracers from his guns in a dead line towards a German plane. Then he climbed away from it as it fell in a spiral, one more scrawl of vapour in the sky.

Then suddenly the air was clear of planes. The sky was vast and empty, although urgent voices still crackled through his headphones. And for one desperate moment away from the combat, for a moment he remembered Nancy. The thought of her lit his mind like a beautiful star. But only for a moment.

There were planes around him again.

He went back to the battle.

Paul stood in front of Wing Commander Vines who was busy for a moment with papers on his desk. Disciplinary Warrant Officer Wiles stood sternly in the background. The hole in the wall that Perce's Chook Chariot had made, was now repaired. It had been a pretty big hole.

"Well, Paul," said the CO, looking up at last. "We've all been here before, haven't we?"

"Yes, sir."

"Last time it was the Air Force who upset public property and disturbed the civilians."

"Yes," said the boy.

"Now the picture's different, isn't it?"

"Yes."

"What's the background, DWO?"

DWO Wiles marched forward and saluted. They'd worked it out beforehand. It would be impressive and regimental.

"On the night of fifteenth instant said boy did release a flock of sheep into the woolshed dance at the property

77

of Mrs Marchington Moss and did cause alarm and despondency, upsetting a number of people, a bowl of punch and most of all, the person of Mrs Moss . . . sir!''

"That's a pretty serious charge, Paul."

"Yes."

"DWO, on the previous occasion when we were at fault, what transpired?"

The DWO saluted again: "Said guilty party one LAC Grice now posted overseas was grounded for a fortnight and did proceed to pigsty at the property of Mrs Sims and did clean same under supervision of Defendant Paul Sims."

"I might add, sir," said DWO Wiles, "the boy was very hard on him. Very strict, sir."

"I see," said Wing Commander Vines, surveying his pencil and the red-faced boy in front of him. "Then I think it would be proper if, in this case, the civilian in question performed an appropriate punishment."

"Justice," said that humbug DWO Wiles, "should not only be done but should be seen to be done."

"Isn't that fair, lad?" said the CO to Paul.

"Yes, that's fair," he said. He wondered what the punishment would be.

"Send in Sergeant Hopson, DWO."

Sergeant Hopson entered and saluted. He was the biggest person Paul had ever seen, the floorboards creaked as he walked and he stamped to attention bringing his huge muscular arm to a nippy salute.

"Sergeant Hopson is the head cook. Sergeants have dishes to wash, isn't that so, sergeant?"

78

"That's right, sir. Dishes as high as the roof, pots and pans sir, and the soup boiler sir, mustn't forget the soup boiler."

"Big is it, sergeant?" They had carefully rehearsed it all.

"Big as a railway engine, sir."

"I'm assigning Paul Sims to you for an hour, sergeant. He's paying off a debt of honour, mind you. Firmness, sergeant, rather than any sort of victimisation."

"I wouldn't victimise anyone," said Sergeant Hopson. "I'm a gentle soul. I'm just fussy, sir. About grease and little specks that might get inside men's stomachs. So I make people scrub pots until their hands bleed and their heads wobble. But I'm a just man and a kind man. Away from my kitchen I'm as gentle as a kitten."

Paul had never seen any kitten like Sergeant Hopson. Or tiger either.

There were boiling pots all right and roaring stoves. There were messmen and cooks and great dirty pans. It was more like a factory than a kitchen. And there was Sergeant Hopson, enormous and efficient, now wearing a vast apron and very much at home among his kingdom of stoves and saucepans and potato peelers.

"This is where we put fuel in the human tanks," he bellowed at Paul who was already scrubbing a vast pan. "This is where the boys are turned into men. There are five hundred hungry men out there, lad. This is what puts the stuffing into them. Scrub up, you've only just started."

He seemed to take a great delight in his task. He gave it a fine, theatrical flourish. "Teach the boy a lesson but not too hard a one," the CO had said. "He's a nice kid and he'll thank us for it one day. There's a problem about his sister and one of our airmen and the boy's sensitive about it."

"Who's the lad?" asked an interested cook.

"This lad is Paul Sims who messed up the woolshed dance. I was dancing with Emmy Smithers," said the sergeant. "You know Emmy Smithers at the co-op store. You must know Emmy. She's a neat little number. Feet like a fairy and just as she's snuggling closer and looking into my eyes she gives a scream . . ."

"Go on," said the listener, all agog.

"Next thing she's carried away on a sheep's back. A sheep introduced by a recalcitrant civilian and none other than this freckled potscrubber here. So work on it, lad. This is on behalf of my friend Emmy Smithers who is home with a sprained ankle brought on by a bleating Merino ewe hunted in by an irresponsible whippersnapper."

Paul went red around the ears and scrubbed on. "I'm taking my medicine," he said.

"Medicine, lad, medicine will taste like ginger beer, castor oil like honey ice cream, alongside what I got for you next. The next pan is so big you'll have to row out in it. On a clear day you can just see the other side. Only on a clear day, mind you."

Another pot was dragged forward. "Go to work, lad," said Sergeant Hopson. He noticed a grinning corporal nearby.

"Hey," he said. "Come here, Corporal Hines. Now

lad, meet Corporal Hines. Smartest cook in the service. Beautiful uniform. That right, corporal?"

"That's right, sergeant."

"He's standing by the punch bowl, lad. Watching the passing parade at the woolshed. A man who cooks hard for the services. Having a little leisure and what happens? He's knocked backwards by a great Merino ram with a head like concrete. And he's drenched in punch. Drenched. His new uniform torn and ruined. Can't even go on leave to see his Mum. That right, corporal?"

"That's right, sergeant," said Corporal Hines.

"I'm sorry," the boy said.

"The world's full of people being sorry," said the sergeant, sighing hugely.

The next moment he was sorry himself. Paul saw a remarkable change of expression on Sergeant Hopson's face—incredulity, embarrassment, respect. The sergeant leapt suddenly to a quivering, mountainous attention.

"Stand easy," said a voice behind the boy. "Now what's this? We're recruiting some very young messmen, I see."

Paul turned. There was a small group of officers—Wing Commander Vines looking a little sheepish and among the others a tall, obviously very senior, officer, the one who was doing the talking.

"Oh me gawd, the Grouper," moaned a cook somewhere.

"Just making an inspection," said the group captain. "Keeps the Wings on their toes, eh Vines? What's your name, lad?"

"Paul."

"Why are you scrubbing pots?"

"It is punishment."

"For what?" The group captain's eyebrows lifted slightly.

"I messed up their dance," said Paul. "Let the sheep in."

The CO explained.

"A bit irregular isn't it, Vines? The whole thing not quite King's regulations?"

A little embarrassed silence ensued.

"Keeping the boy at it, are you sergeant?" asked the Grouper to Sergeant Hopson.

"As much as I can, sir," said Sergeant Hopson.

"You might keep some of your other staff at it too. I've seen cleaner kitchens," said the Grouper. "And tidier cooks. You'll look to that, sergeant."

"Yes, sir."

The group captain paused a moment before leaving: "Well Paul, I hope you don't let any more sheep into any more dances. Dancing and sheep don't mix."

"I won't do it again," said Paul.

"Carry on," said the group captain and saluted.

Some of the authority seemed to go out of Sergeant Hopson. In fact it blew out like a pricked balloon. A messman rushed him a cup of tea.

"Bring one for the boy, too. He's finished his jobs," said the sergeant. "Life's hard in the Services, lad. We got some very sneaky officers. Always snooping around the station spying on us poor cooks. Criticising my kitchen which is as clean as a new pin. Isn't that so, Corporal Hines?"

"That's right, sergeant," said the corporal.

"And bring the boy some biscuits," the sergeant said. He looked even more ferocious when he was being friendly.

As a driver took Paul home he saw another part of Air Force life. A Tiger Moth tipped over on its wings after it landed and then crumpled like a broken toy. The fire tender, ambulance and other vehicles raced toward it. Someone was helping the pilot from the cockpit. He was obviously hurt but not too badly.

There was a spurt of flame at the plane but a quick flurry of foam from the fire tender with its goggled figures wearing protective clothing.

"Lucky that time," said the driver, who'd pulled up for a moment.

As they drove off along the road to home Paul noticed another hawk about. It was a big bird, slow and majestic. But he must remember to tell Curtiss. Big hawks meant trouble for poultry and for pigeons too.

And it made him think. The war was like a hawk, its great shadow drifting over them all.

10. An Echo of Guns

Jody was waiting for him when he returned from the Air Force station.

"What was it like?" she asked.

He told her. He didn't tell Nancy about the plane crash because he thought it would worry her. But he gave a vivid description of the mess sergeant and the dish-washing.

"You've learnt your lesson I hope, Paul," his mother said. She seemed to have other worries. "Curtiss, I think, is having one of his bad times."

Paul knew what that meant.

"Speak to him, Paul," Nancy said. "I think the war news has upset him. It's bad again."

It always was, Paul thought.

Jody looked concerned. She liked Curtiss. She was so much a part of this family and Curtiss was family too, in a way.

Jody realised that she lived on a prosperous farm, that she was lucky with her parents and she felt a little guilty when she saw how the Sims family had to struggle sometimes.

"Shall we go and talk to Curtiss? Cheer him up," she said in her forthright, helpful way.

"Hadn't you better go home, Jody," said Mrs Sims. "Not that we don't like you here. But your mother says she never sees you."

"Particularly at job time," said Nancy. She gave the girl a hug. It was her brother, that tousle-headed, affectionate troublemaker, that this girl really liked. A nice independent spirit was Jody.

"Say hullo to Curtiss, anyway." Curtiss was one of the family props with his meticulous farming. His dark times concerned them all.

Curtiss was leaning on the gate when Jody and Paul approached. It was an old gate, a bit lopsided on its hinges. Curtiss oiled them but they squeaked still. He liked leaning on the gate. He could look across the countryside to the west, to the line of the river trees where the white cockatoos flapped and screeched in an awkward crowd, to the distant huddle of buildings and trees that was the township. When he felt low he came here and smoked his pipe. The sight of the land comforted him.

"Hullo, Curtiss," they said.

He turned his head slowly. He looked tired.

"You do your job at the Air Force?"

"Yes," Paul said.

"He did it OK. He took his medicine. A group captain came and everyone was embarrassed. And a plane cracked up, but the pilot wasn't hurt too badly."

Jody was quick with the news.

Curtiss looked away again. He jerked his pipestem at the west.

"Bad weather coming." He looked gloomy. A crow

85

lodged on an old dead tree nearby and made a dreary sound, as cheerless as the sky.

"Must chop that tree down one day for wood," Curtiss said. "I don't like dead trees. I saw a lot of dead trees once. In France. I don't like dead trees."

He was quiet again, drawing on his pipe. Soon, Paul thought, Curtiss will go back to his neat little room and get on the grog and be sad and Tops will howl and the mouth organ will start. That was the way it went.

Jody said goodbye and Paul walked with her to her horse.

"Curtiss looks tired," she said.

"Thanks for coming today," said Paul, putting his hand on the saddle. He enjoyed her company. Whether she was a tomboy or not she was loyal and stood up for her friends. And she was nice to Nancy.

She was off with a wave and then, knowing he was watching, she sent her horse into a gallop, leaning low over its neck and feeling the excitement of the onrushing ride.

"Show-off," Paul thought.

Then he went back to Curtiss.

The man was pointing to a little glowing patch in the sky, a trick of light like an oval rainbow perched on the corner of a cloud.

"That's a sun dog," said Curtiss. "Always means bad weather."

"Mum wants you to have dinner with us tonight." She'd told him and he just remembered it.

"Not tonight. I'll eat at my place tonight, lad. Thank her anyway."

Curtiss walked slowly away with his limp more pronounced than usual.

Paul heard the thunder in the night and saw the curtains of his room lit up by the lightning. He thrust open the window and the rain was drumming over the paddocks with an increasing roar until it swept down on the farm, hammering the roofs and flooding the gutters. The thunder came again and the lightning was bright and by its glare the boy saw a frightening sight.

Curtiss was out in the yard by the stable, without a coat, flinging his arms about, the rain beating on him. The lightning came and went. There was one fiery flash, the splintering of a tree, the crash as a branch struck the stable roof, and the screams of the horses.

The noise of the horses seemed to send Curtiss crazy. He was half running, half staggering into the stables and then he was among the plunging horses.

The boy was out through his bedroom window. He raced barefooted into the rain-lashed night, water dripping down his nose and running down his back.

"Curtiss," the boy shouted but the storm swept his words away. He still hammered them out. "Curtiss, Curtiss."

The white blazes on the faces of the horses were ghostly in the flashes of lightning. Their eyes were rimmed with the white of terror. The man was among them wandering crazily among the rearing, plunging hoofs. Then he stumbled and fell.

The boy was through the fence and at his side, calling to

the horses as he did. "Whoa, boys, back boys, back whoa."

He began dragging Curtiss through the stable yard, across the wet manure, afraid the big hoofs might strike him. He saw the great branch of the tree thrust through the stable roof, some of the straw and iron collapsing, the spear of a broken beam. At last he got Curtiss out of the yard and dragged and pulled him through the door of the chaff shed that adjoined the stable, both of them saturated, the man seeming half unconscious, moaning. Inside the chaff shed was mostly intact although the rain beat through the shattered roof further along.

"Curtiss, Curtiss," he said. He grabbed a bag of chaff and propped up the man's head. There was a terrifying clap of thunder, the lightning bright as day.

Curtiss sat bolt upright, a terrible expression on his face, and began shouting.

"They're shelling the horses. They're killing the horses. The bastards are shelling the horses."

Then the boy knew that Curtiss was back in time, back in the old war, back at the front. It was all buried deep in his mind and now it was coming out. The beer and the storm and the pain in his leg that came with a change of weather, and the raking, terrifying memory was with him, consuming him.

"I've got you, Curtiss," Paul said. "It's all right. It's the storm, a branch broke off and frightened the horses."

"What, boy, what?" Curtiss stirred and shook his head. "Where are we?"

"In the chaff shed."

"What are you doing out of bed?"

"I heard the lightning hit the tree and you were crawling around in the stable."

A light came at the chaff shed door. It was Paul's mother, Nancy behind with a lantern. "What happened? What's up?"

Curtiss sat up.

"Sorry, missus. I guess I had a bit too much. Thunder and the storm and the horses. Like a bad dream. The horses screaming. Like a bad dream."

Nancy, big as she was, came and knelt beside him.

"I know," she said. "You must have some bad memories, Curtiss. Come to the house and we'll make a cup of tea."

"You shouldn't be out in the wet," the boy said to his sister.

"And what are you doing, barefooted and drenched and teeth clattering like knucklebones?"

"He must have hauled me from the stable yard," Curtiss said. "I must have been a bit far gone."

"It's all right, Curtiss," Mrs Sims said. "We understand." The storm rumbled away and the rain eased. Paul opened one of the windows through which he put chaff into the mangers. Beyond in the yard the horses were still trembling. But they pricked up their ears at the sound of the window's opening. Their appetites conquered their fear and they thrust their soft noses into the manger and began to eat, blowing their noses with contentment into the chaff.

"Good lad, that'll quieten them," said Curtiss, getting

to his feet and once more in control of himself.

Later in the house they all sat around the freshly built fire and drank tea and made toast.

"Curtiss," said Nancy. "Would you like to talk about it?"

He talked for a bit because he seemed glad to have his friends around him by the fire. Paul's mother moved discreetly while he talked to the listening girl and the boy who'd shown such pluck out there in the yard.

He started to talk: "It was the screams of the horses."

And then he stopped and thought: How can I tell them?

How can I tell them about the noise of the shells, the great gouts of mud, your heart beating as if it was about to leap out of your body, the terror to find cover, pressing yourself down in a shellhole, mud in your mouth, the barbed wire ripping your clothes, the splintered fangs of the tree trunks around you?

And the horses struggling, struggling up to their bellies, the terrible ripple and stretch of their muscles in the mud, their ears bent back, and your shoulders against the wheels of the gun carriages, the guns cold and metallic. And then flinging yourself down again with your mouth full of filth and mud, mud, mud.

And it all came back to him across the years, across the scarred reaches of his mind where nothing could quite heal it, not even time.

"Curtiss," the boy said, but Nancy hushed him, watching the man's wet, tired face, with a tenderness beyond her years.

Curtiss didn't hear the boy. He was hearing other voices

saying when he came home, "You came back, but he didn't" and saying it accusingly because they were weighed down with grief. This girl he'd known and liked, he was with her brother, the brother they'd left behind. They were all like the earth now, the ones left behind.

That was why he liked farming. The earth healed things. It covered the awful things and the crops grew again. The hedges and the birds came back and the flowers.

That's why he liked farming because you were on your own and the earth was there and when you turned the earth you did it with a plough and not a bloody great gun.

The furrows were neat and beautiful and straight and the wheat came up in its splendid rows and the hares came into it and there was nothing twisted and dead about.

"Curtiss, are you all right?" There were Nancy and Paul looking at him with concern.

"You did all right calming the horses, Paul, and hauling me out," Curtiss said. "Won't happen again, lad. I'd best be off to bed."

"Like me to come with you?" Paul said.

"What, and tuck in me toes? No lad, you get some sleep. And you too Nancy, you got to be careful—you got two to think about, Nancy. Thanks for the tea, missus. In fact, thanks for everything . . . all of you."

He went slowly out the door into the night. The stars had come out again and the thunder was a faint growl in the distance and the lightning a mere malignant flicker far on the horizon. Nancy put her arm around Paul and he felt her tremble.

91

11. Drive Through the Night

An hour later the baby began to come.

Mrs Sims picked up the telephone but it made that crackling irritable sound of a telephone out of order.

"It's the storm," she said frantically.

"I'll run across to Jody's," Paul said. "It's not far. They'll have their car."

"They can't. It's in the garage being fixed," Nancy said. Her face was white with pain.

"I'll run," said the boy and he was out of the door and into the night, splashing through the water left by the storm which had so quickly receded, leaving the stars to come out sharp and white and the air full of the smell of washed earth. He was through the fence and along the well-worn path that led to Jody's home. He knew the path with eyes shut. He saw the loom of the house ahead. He ran quickly, slipping a little on the muddy path, his mind busy with the message. The town with the hospital was some miles away.

"Ring Perce," his mother had shouted. "His car's fixed now. Ring Perce, get Jody's mother to ring Perce."

"Yes," he shouted over his shoulder and he was through another fence and then over a gate and soon into the yard of the other farmhouse.

It didn't seem to take long slipping and sliding and scrambling in his alarm and eagerness.

The family's dogs came rushing out baying with alarm. Lights went on, a lantern swaying suddenly.

"Who's there?"

"It's Paul. Nancy's having the baby. We've got to ring Perce for his car."

Paul took deep breaths between the words as they rushed out.

"We've got to ring Perce quickly."

Jody was there and her mother and father.

"Paul, the storm's put out the telephone. There's a line down somewhere."

"I'll get my clothes on and get the horse." It was Jody quick as a flash.

"The road's slippery," her father said. "I'll harness the buggy."

"Too long and too slow," the girl said, taking charge. "Trimmer's in his stall." She raced away for her clothes.

She was back in seconds, it seemed.

"Watch the road," her mother was shouting. "It's dangerous. Here Paul, grab the lantern and open the gate."

Jody's father was running to the stable to saddle her horse. The horse whinnied, sensing the excitement and the unusual activities. The dogs went on barking in that hap-hazard way that changes from warning and threat to sociable barking as if enquiring what the fuss was and could they be of help.

Paul said, "I can't just wait here. I'll have to go back."

"We'll come with you," said Mrs Carson. Mr Carson

was leading the saddled horse. Jody with her coat on was in the saddle with one quick movement, the boy running to open the gate for her.

Then she was riding into the night, riding with concentration, low over the horse's flying mane but watching the wet road in the moonlight which now flooded the countryside, the mud spattering in her face as she splashed through it, her horse responding to her urgency, keeping its sure footing, feeling the touch of rein and knee as she skirted a pool of water, using the sandy verges of the road where it wasn't slippery and then coming on to the metalled sections where the horse's hoofs rang in urgent rhythm, echoing away into the night.

Perce heard the horse coming licketty-split. The storm had woken him and frightened his Orpingtons nearly to death and he was making his last rounds to see that the fowlhouse door was shut against the foxes. He had dislodged a couple of fowls from his car and guided them firmly to their roost. He was pleased about the car. The Air Force had done a good job with the renovations. It roared like a racer and seemed young again.

The rider was pulling up, the girl Jody running towards him, dragging the horse behind her after she'd slid off with a smooth, quick movement.

"We've got to have your car. Nancy's baby's coming. We've got to get her to hospital."

Perce broke into a run for his house with the girl coming behind him. Inside he grabbed an old coat, his wallet with his driving licence (he never went anywhere without the driving licence although no one ever asked him for it) and then he started searching for the danged key of the car.

"I put it down on the table," he said, turning up the lamp.

"Where?" cried Jody. "Where?" The table was a disorganised mess of old dishes and opened tins with a huge mutton bone, stringy and the size of a bullock's leg and obviously meant for one of the dogs.

Perce began agitatedly brushing the tins on the floor in his haste and they clattered and banged and the dogs outside began barking and the poultry cackling.

"Here it is," shouted Jody. "Hurry up. I'll put my horse in your yard and come with you, Perce. I hope your car starts."

Paul was standing at the gate post at home, watching the township road. He saw a pair of lights coming and they were coming at speed. As the car turned into the lane he could see it was Perce. He had the gate opened and jumped on the running board as Perce went past.

Jody was there too. "I left my horse at Perce's," she shouted. "I'm coming too."

Paul's mother and Mrs Carson had everything ready and helped Nancy into the back of the car and Mrs Sims climbed in beside her.

Paul who was dressed now said, "I'm coming too."

"And so am I," said Jody.

"Children, you'd better stay here." Mrs Carson looked startled.

"I'm going with Nancy," said the boy.

"Let him come," said Nancy and gave a little gasp of pain, "and hurry please."

Paul sprang into the front seat and Jody squeezed beside him, Nancy tucked up in the blankets in the back with her mother, then the old car started off with a terrible roar, every shuddering piston working to capacity. The little group to see them off went backward into the night—Mr and Mrs Carson, Curtiss who had joined the group and Tops.

"Thank goodness for the Air Force," said Jody. "They've put an aeroplane engine in it."

Perce just sat there, big and earnest and worried about the bumpy road and glaring at the yellow spots the headlights threw on the road.

They were all sitting in the little waiting room of the local hospital, Perce in his rough old clothes, Paul still with mud on his face from his sprint across the paddock and back, Jody muddy from her ride and Mrs Sims anxious and sipping tea.

They all had a cup of tea. A thoughtful nurse had brought it while the drama went on, the scurrying of the night staff, the hurried arrival of the doctor.

"Heavens," he said. "The whole family. Don't worry, she's a fine strong girl and she'll be all right."

Then matron appeared, regal and unruffled, the night sister in a white gown, once a little cry from somewhere in the hospital which made Paul clutch his cup and Jody move a little closer to him.

Somewhere a patient was snoring and it went on monotonously among all the tumult.

It had an effect on Perce and Paul. One was getting old

and found it hard driving in the night with all the tension and responsibility and the other was suffering from too much running and anxiety.

Paul struggled to keep his eyes open as time dragged along but his eyelids shuttered down in the persistent onset of sleep.

Finally his head fell heavily against Jody's shoulder and she smiled a little at the feel of it. Finally she put her arm around him because he would have fallen off the seat.

"Men," said Mrs Sims. "Look at them both."

For Perce was sleeping too.

It seemed a long time before the nurse came to the anxious woman and the wakeful girl. The other two still slept.

Paul dreamed of aeroplanes and thunder and flying horses until someone shook him awake.

He focused on the white uniform of the matron and the happy, tired face of Jody who still had her arm around him.

"Wake up, uncle," said Jody. "You've a nephew."

"Where are we?" said Perce, waking with a start and staring at the populated, gleaming white room so different from his old, congested bedroom with clothes hanging over chairs and underwear on the floor.

Then it all came back. "How's Nancy?"

"Nancy's fine. It's a boy."

"It's a boy," said Perce. "Well I never, it's a boy."

As though it was the first boy who had ever been born.

12. The Time of the Hawk

The baby changed the life of the household and even Tops the dog seemed to know it.

The baby Ian's shrill cries, his antics, the bathing, the mealtimes became the centre around which the household revolved.

Sometimes the child would lie quietly and Paul tried to think who it was like but it looked like nothing he had ever seen before.

Paul didn't mind particularly as Nancy was happy again, happy because letters came from John Grice and from his parents, and this made her happy and set her singing and seemed to relieve Mrs Sims's mind too.

The letters were important and when he went to collect the mail there was always a tense, anxious little crowd waiting at the post office with geranium pots on its counter and the lattice with the creeper by the little post office window.

"Letters for Nancy, Paul, from overseas," said Mrs Postlegate, the thin, sympathetic postmistress. She knew what letters from overseas meant. People would stand around reading them—fathers and mothers and wives and sisters, leaning against posts or sitting in their cars or their buggies, not wanting to drive another yard before they knew how things were in foreign places where their men were serving—in gritty desert camps, in ships on rough cold seas, in dreary bases far away at the war.

Nancy would always be waiting when Paul came cycling home and he'd be waving the letter in his hand before he'd reached the gate because Nancy would be watching and come running down the lane. And then she'd open it on the spot, devouring its lines with her eyes. He'd watch, leaning his bike against the post.

It was the same this day.

"Is John OK?"

"Yes, he's fine. I told him about the christening. That we were having it and maybe some people would disapprove and he's very happy about it."

She went on talking about when John came home, what they'd do, making plans, wistful, happy plans. Everyone talked about coming home. Everyone made plans.

"When they come home . . ." it had drifted around the post office verandah. The boy became aware of the separation the people suffered, the cruel distance.

One day Jody and he were at the railway station when a troop train pulled in. Soldiers leant from the windows, one or two waving letters and saying, "Hey kids, post these."

The last links, these letters, some with pencilled addresses. Jody and Paul had run along grabbing them, and then with a jerk and clatter of couplings and the clack of wheels, the train began to move. Faster it went. A few more letters were tossed out.

Then all the men began to wave. Their faces and arms became a speeding blur . . . "Going to the war," one shouted . . . "Going away . . . away . . ." The rhythm and noise of the train seized and drowned the words and the faces became merged and indistinct as if they had already passed into another dimension, another time.

Then the train was gone with just the boy and girl watching it speed into the distance. Then they took the letters to the post office.

A few days before the christening Paul took his pigeon to the school for a pet show. Miss Ginson the teacher had arranged it to help raise pennies for the war effort.

It wasn't a terribly successful show. Freddie Nilson's guinea pig smelt to high heaven. Philip Riley's dog chased Joanne Winter's cat around the classroom and pandemonium broke out when another cat sprang on little Bessie Miller's white mouse and Miss Ginson decided that enough was enough and sent everyone home early because it was a Friday anyway.

Paul carried his pigeon in a small cage. He'd walked to school because his bike had a puncture and anyway he enjoyed walking with the pigeon murmuring in its box, the slow pleasant walk on a bright Australian day with the paddocks wide and the hares plump and watchful.

Now Jody walked home with him, leading her horse.

"Shall we let it fly?" asked Jody. "It's been cooped up all the morning."

They took the pigeon from its cage and Jody nursed it, the bird sitting quietly in her hands.

"She's grown to like you, Paul," she said.

"Fly pigeon, fly," shouted Jody and the bird rose from her hands in a great wheeling circle, sweeping back over them and getting its direction.

"She knows the way," said Paul. They watched it speeding away and neither of them saw the hawk. It was the big hawk, the newcomer to the area and it hovered high, its keen eyes sweeping the countryside, its instinct sorting out in its beaked head the messages that would send it dropping like a stone on its prey.

At last came the moment it had been waiting for. The wings dipped and the bird went down in a dive, its fierce eyes on the object below, its talons extending.

The pigeon with sudden instinct had turned at the last minute in its flight, a last second that momentarily saved it. The feathered projectile of the hawk went past, but then with all the miraculous and instinctive working of the feathers and wings and tail that steered and propelled it, it came back in frenzied pursuit.

"It's the hawk," shouted Paul, but there was nothing he could do, watching the dark arrow aiming down on the little speck of the bird, the sudden frantic turning towards them. The hawk struck the pigeon not far from Paul and Jody.

It tumbled out of the sky into a limp heap on the fallow. The hawk, alarmed now, flew off. Paul rushed to the little pathetic bundle and picked it up in his hands.

He squatted on his haunches, Jody beside him.

"You'll be able to get another one," she said. She knew how fond he was of the bird.

"I'm sorry about it," she said, "It was so quick and there was nothing we could do."

Jody waited. Paul still ruffled the bird's plumage with

his hand, feeling the softness of the downy feathers of its neck.

"Bury it in the fallow, the ground's soft there," she said gently. He thought to himself, I wonder if the crops will grow a little greener. A pigeon's so small.

"OK," he said. "We'll bury it here."

They did it quickly.

They forgot about the pigeon when they reached Paul's home, when his mother came out sad-faced and behind her Curtiss, clearing his throat as he always did when he was upset about something.

"Where's Nancy?" asked Paul. "Where is she? What's up?"

"We had a message from one of John's Air Force friends."

"About John?" Jody asked.

"About John. He was shot down. He's dead, children."

"Where's Nancy? *Where is she?*" Paul shouted it.

"She took the baby for a walk along the creek. She's taking it very bravely. Paul, Paul, you must leave her alone."

But he was running, his legs going up and down of their own accord, because he was confused, shocked and worried for his sister. He was wondering what to do and what to say. He fell over a log and climbed to his feet again not pausing to dust his knees. Funny things jumped into his mind. Curtiss saying, "Grass withers. New grass grows." Why should he think of a funny thing like that? But he began muttering it, his mouth dry and now he was near to tears because he could see Nancy holding the baby and walking slowly.

102

When he ran to her she was holding the baby against her tightly like a shield, a small warm shield against the reality that she must now face. The boy understood something of it but even he could not comprehend the full anguish. He tried hard. He put a grubby hand on her arm, "Sis, I'm sorry, Sis. I'm sorry."

There was something that was more than sadness in her face. It was the look he'd seen when the aeroplane with John had flown past that day. She was away somewhere.

"Hullo Tiger, don't talk. Just walk with me," she said. "Ian's asleep. Don't talk."

He walked beside her, troubled and concerned and expecting tears but not finding them, though the remains of them were on her cheeks.

He tried to understand it. It was like the pigeon and the hawk. But it was more than that. Nancy walked on and he walked with her and the baby slept.

The sheep moved as they always did, in restless clumps or the clumps breaking into single lines towards the trough. Magpies sang as they always did. The nearby windmill spun and clacked and the water from the bore came out in a clear spurting stream with each movement of the pump down the pipe. The ants ran about on their tiny tracks as they always did.

And the wind came to bend the reeds in the little pools in the creek, parting them and laying them back in a soft rustle, while the two figures on the bank went slowly by and the baby stirred a little in the arms of its mother.

And Paul thought: How could there be death on a day like this?

13. *The Guiding Light*

The christening was going ahead.

Nancy told them she wanted it that way. Nobody changed her mind, nobody could and nobody wanted to. Paul had been as attentive and helpful as he could since the news of John's death and Jody had been over to talk and to help wash the baby who was now nearly three months old. The Air Force had been kind and so had neighbours. But some people still talked; some people were still cool about the child and there was no word of condolence from Mrs Marchington Moss; she had her own son to worry about, Mrs Sims said in her kind way.

The weather was dry again and becoming warm, the winter had been poor and feed was scarce in the paddocks.

Aunt Rosa had come to stay and she was worse than the dry winter, more miserable than toothache, as complaining as an east wind and a proper cheer-up to have about the house. She tried to be helpful, but succeeded only in being disapproving. Paul and Aunt Rosa were never the best of friends and quarrelled during the washing up and he was reprimanded by his mother and even by Curtiss.

Nancy was pale but composed. She went for long walks by the creek with the baby. Even Paul didn't intrude now. He knew these were her moments, her away-somewhere times. He thought of her now.

"Well, a penny for your thoughts," said the loud voice of Jody. She was standing on the shafts of the dray which she was driving and staring up at him pitching off dry sheaves at intervals along the paddock for the sheep. Curtiss had carefully husbanded the hay but he reckoned the sheep needed a bit of dry stuff as he put it, so Paul was dropping the sheaves in a long line, the wind skittering the bits of straw away.

"Just thinking."

"About Nancy?"

"Yep."

"I think about her too," she said in her concerned way. "It will be a bit of a struggle for your mother and everyone."

"We'll manage."

"I know you will. And I'll help."

"You're driving crooked, watch out," Paul said.

"Hey, I haven't seen the big hawk lately," Jody said, straightening the horse. "Perhaps someone shot it."

"Hawks have a right to live, I s'pose," he said. But he missed his pigeon.

The sun slipped down as they went back to the barn with its adjoining stable. Paul unhitched the horse after he'd backed the dray under the lean-to attached to the shed.

He went to the barn to light the lantern, giving it a good shake first to see that it had plenty of kerosene, which it did. Then he lit it, the yellow light faltering as he adjusted the wick. Then he lowered the glass and the lantern burnt steadily, throwing long crooked shadows in the chaff shed.

The darkness was coming quickly. Outside objects were losing their distinctness, landmarks were blurs in the gloom.

"Listen," said Jody. "Hear it. It's a plane quite low."

"It's too low," he said urgently. "Sounds like a Tiger Moth. It can't reach the drome that low."

They listened again; the plane noise faded and then came back more strongly.

"I reckon he's circling, he's lost," Paul said. "He's looking for a landing all right."

"He'll crash," the girl said. "Hey," she added, Paul had suddenly driven the pitchfork into a sheaf of hay. He picked up the lantern carefully and unscrewed its stopper and sprinkled some kerosene on the sheaf. He was careful with it. He knew about fires in haysheds.

The girl knew what he intended to do. "Don't light it here," she said urgently. "Out in the paddock."

Then she picked up the lantern and he grabbed the fork with the sheaf speared on it and they raced for the paddock. The plane circled again, the pilot obviously trying to sort out a landing place in the fading light, made more treacherous by a lack of wind and a dusty haze that swam close to the ground.

So they ran through the fence and then on, side by side, the plane circling lower and lower. They reached the first of the line of sheaves in the field. Paul lit the sheaf on the fork and it burst into a bright flame. "I'll run back and put the lantern on the post. It'll show the fence line," the girl shouted.

But the boy was running with the sheaf, applying it to

the tinder-dry sheaves of hay like a torch and then racing
to the next sheaf and to the next in an untidy line across the
paddock.

The breathless girl came racing back, catching him up.

The pilot must have seen the pinpoint of the lantern and
then the tiny spurts of flame as the sheaves began to burn
until the makeshift flare path lit up in a ragged line, the
flickering tongues of flame penetrating the dusk.

"It's coming in to land," Jody shrieked. There was a
humming, whistling sound in the air and the plane swept
out of the night like a great unsteady bird, its wheels nearly
knocking the lantern off the post.

"Lie down, Jody," Paul shouted, grabbing her by the
shoulder and they flung themselves flat as the plane
bumped past them and a wing swept over them like a giant
scythe while the slipstream sent a great shower of burning
sparks from the straw in a wild dance like a thousand
fireflies.

The girl and boy lay there a moment, both of them
breathing heavily at the sudden furious action and the terrible nearness of the plane's wings as it passed them. The
plane careered down the paddock, its speed dropping and
at the last moment the pilot slewed it around and it tilted
over on its nose for a moment, and pieces of its broken propeller sang through the air and sent Jody and Paul ducking
again. Then it settled on an even keel again as the two
raced up. Other people were coming too from the house
with a waving lantern and a yelping dog.

The pilot clambered out of the plane, shining a torch on
the damaged propeller. Then he saw the girl and the boy.

For a moment the flashlight shone on them. "You two," said the voice, "the last time I saw you, Paul, you were messing up my mother's woolshed dance. A flare path of hay. Well, you saved me and my plane, bless you and your quick wits."

Then Nancy arrived, and Curtiss and Tops.

"I'm all right," said Philip Marchington Moss, "but I'd better ring the station. And I could do with a cup of tea."

"You're not hurt," Nancy said.

"Just a bleeding nose and a bruise the size of a hen's egg on my manly forehead. Pretty lucky, thanks to the pathfinders here."

"Then we'll try some hot water and disinfectant and some good old-fashioned bathing," said Nancy, "and a hot cup of tea."

"Thanks," he said. "And thanks again to you two...."

They all walked to the house. Nancy and the young pilot ahead, the boy and the girl behind and Curtiss and Tops bringing up the rear. Curtiss looked back at the smouldering remnants of hay. He'd seen hay put to some strange uses, but this beat them all.

It was the christening day, Sunday morning.

Paul had been up early feeding the horses so that everything would be ready.

"Wouldn't you like to come to the christening?" he said through the manger window to Prince the chestnut, the big slow reliable furrow horse, but Prince blew chaff from his

108

nostrils and seemed only interested in breakfast.

"Wouldn't you like to go to the christening, Tops?" he said to the dog who had swung his tail to show his interest.

Paul's mother had risen early too to see to some final cooking, "in case anyone wanted to come back to the house afterwards."

And Aunt Rosa, the State's leading wet blanket, was full of gloom, woe-betiding and mark-my-wording.

"People won't come," she said. Aunt Rosa was calamity on two thin legs. Even in good times she found things to complain about and in sad times she cast about her in a feverish melancholy, not knowing which piece of bad news to discuss first.

"It's a beautiful day, and Ian has had a good breakfast."

They all turned towards Nancy. She was pale but calm, the baby in her arms. The baby seemed contented enough. Even Aunt Rosa admitted that.

"I hope you're not overfeeding him. I've seen babies fed until it runs out of their ears."

"Nothing will run out of his pink ears," Nancy said. "And you'd better be careful, aunty. He hears a lot with them already. Hullo Paul, have you done your jobs?"

"He's been up early," this from Curtiss who had also come up for breakfast. "Up early without so much as a shake. Never been known before."

"The Air Force haven't been to collect their plane yet," Nancy indicated it through the window.

"They're sending mechanics to fix the propeller," Paul said.

109

"You'd better take some tea to the sentry. He must be cold," Mrs Sims said. The Air Force had sent two guards. One was still asleep in the hayhouse when he took a billy of tea, cups and some toast buttered and wrapped in a cloth to keep warm.

"Hullo chief," said the Air Force guard, sitting up in the straw. "Nice of your mother to send the tea. I feel like it. Then I'll relieve LAC Moon out there guarding the aircraft with his trusty musket. He's probably a bit peckish too. Big day, eh?"

The guard had heard about the christening.

"Yes it is."

"People get worked up about christenings," the guard said. "About what they're going to call the kids. Families get hurt if they don't get a mention in the kid's name. Know what my second name is? Aloysius."

"It's not a bad name," Paul said.

"Thank God it's only my second name," said the guard.

At that moment Curtiss came in. "Jody's riding up," he said. "She's early, isn't she?"

The guard seemed very learned about christenings: "When you've got a christening the women flock around like bees. Well, they have the children so it's their right I reckon."

The guard picked up his rifle and a piece of toast.

"Well, I'll relieve poor old shivering LAC Moon."

He winked at Paul, "See they don't call the poor kid Aloysius."

14. A Band Along the Road

The house was getting into an uproar, Paul thought. Curtiss had retired to his little lean-to to wash and put on his best suit.

Perce was coming with his car to pick up the main actors in the day's event. Inside the house Aunt Rosa was hurrying everybody through cups of tea. Her enthusiasm seemed to have awakened at last. Paul's mother was icing a last cake.

Jody was spruced in a sharp dress, her hair shining. She was leaning over Ian, the baby, and Nancy was preparing the christening gown. They were busy and they gave Paul only a fleeting look and then began talking together.

"Why are you here so early, Jody?" Paul asked.

"She's come to help me."

"But I'm here to help."

"Well, you're a marvellous help, Paul, but you'll have to get out of the way so I can get around that side to change him."

Nancy stopped and looked at Paul. She was smiling but her eyes had that somewhere look.

She gave his arm a squeeze: "It's nice just for you to be around, but I do think you might be doing something for mother."

"Yes, don't get in the way, Paul," said Jody.

Paul went to the kitchen just in time to hear Aunt Rosa say: "But a lot of people are still talking and I know it's hard for the girl and there was that business at the wool-shed dance with Paul and I don't think we can really expect people to forget and come along in droves and the girl not married. . . ."

"Mind you don't fall against the stove and burn yourself, Aunt Rosa," Paul said in a loud voice.

"But I'm not near the stove," she said in alarm.

"I'm just telling you, that's all," Paul said.

"That boy needs discipline, he's getting too cheeky."

"Have a cup of tea," Paul said. Aunt Rosa looked surprised and then suspicious.

"Well, I would like another cup. Boiling water now."

Paul noticed something else on the sink by the stove.

"That's kind of you, Paul," she said a few moments later as he poured the tea.

Then he went out.

He heard the exclamation a few moments later: "This tea tastes of soap. Ethel, there's soap in that tea. It's that boy. He did it deliberately. Mark my words."

You're not behaving well, Paul told himself. He looked at the sky and thought of his pigeon and then he thought of John Grice and he looked at the biplane standing in the field, the wind gusting through its wings and struts and a magpie sitting unperturbed on its mainplane. But it was time to have a wash and clean his shoes. He mustn't spoil Nancy's day.

The Chook Chariot was the cleanest it had ever been. Perce had washed it and polished it, swept its floor and covered the seats with a rug.

Paul put on his coat and gave his tie a last tug as the car rolled up outside. Perce had on a collar and tie and his best suit and Curtiss came up, dapper and smelling of eau de cologne. His thinnish hair had a disciplined furrow through it.

They all grouped around the door as Nancy came out carrying the baby. She walked carefully and slowly with Jody following with a blanket, Mrs Sims behind and Aunt Rosa bringing up the rear in a bright red dress that would make a horse bolt. There was a moment's silence. The racket of the windmill slowly turning in the warm air, the cry of the sheep, and the old constant murmur of the pepper tree.

The child in Nancy's arms made a soft, contented sucking sound and opened his enormous blue eyes.

"Look at that," said Perce, and involuntarily took off his hat in admiration.

When they reached the church it seemed as if all the world was there, the world that was the farming district. Older farmers in slightly old-fashioned suits, women in their best. Cars and horses and buggies were parked and tied higgledy-piggledy along the road in their independent country confusion.

Nancy sat straighter in the back of the car when she saw it all. Colour came into her face. Aunt Rosa for once was speechless. Everyone was waiting outside the church including the Reverend Eversley, his dog collar a brilliant starched white.

113

Paul rushed to open the car door for Nancy. He'd come a little ahead with Curtiss in the buggy and Jody had ridden her horse.

"Hold him while I get out," Nancy said. Paul took Ian in his arms and held him like a young grizzly about to crush his first victim, fearful that he might drop Ian in his christening gown.

And then they were all ready, standing there by the small square church with its square windows, with a line of pigeons on the roof, with the pepper trees throwing a fine tracery of shadow on the ground.

Someone came forward, someone they never expected, someone dressed in a great swathe of a dress and with a huge hat and brooches and beads, someone with a white shawl in her hands, someone diffident and ill at ease.

"Nancy," said Mrs Marchington Moss, for it was she. "This was my son's christening shawl. I want you to have it. I'm deeply grateful for all you did for my son and the forced landing and Paul's and Jody's presence of mind. I-I-I..."

Paul and Jody stared in amazement. They felt they were about to see an incredible sight—Mrs Marchington Moss blubbering.

But Nancy in her quick and understanding way, said: "How lovely, Mrs Moss. Will you hold Ian so we can put it around him?"

Gratefully Mrs Marchington Moss held him.

"She knows how to hold kids after all," said Jody.

Paul had heard another sound but he didn't take much

114

notice of it. More people coming he thought, but it sounded like trucks.

Other people heard it. The noise ceased and there was shouting along the road. And then they heard it, all of them, the tuneful swirling sound of a brass band coming along the road. Nancy heard it and lifted her head and the child in her arms heard it and stirred and murmured. The pigeons heard it and stopped cleaning themselves and the Reverend Eversley straightened his dog collar and looked important.

There was a band coming down the road all right, the band from the Air Force station and behind them was the CO with a line of ribbons on his chest and behind him DWO Wiles, immaculate and regimental, and behind him, of all people, the huge bulk of Sergeant Hopson, immaculate too and treading like a ballet dancer. And then a squad of men, arms swinging, boots glistening. In the paddock alongside there was a mad escort of excited cows, tails up, horns tossing, galloping along the fence.

Nancy lifted Ian up to see the procession and held him against her face, but high, and he didn't whimper and Paul reckoned he must have liked the music.

Not everyone got in the church which was packed tighter than a tin of sardines. Regular churchgoers cramped up in their seats to allow some of the Air Force in. When Sergeant Hopson sat down Paul expected the other end of the seat to fly up like a see-saw and propel the people on it through the window. But nothing happened, just a creak. A place was cleared near the front for the CO and DWO Wiles and Mrs Holifer the organist nearly trod the pedals off the instrument, her fingers, chafed from milking countless cows, now chasing Christian soldiers onwards down the old yellowing keys.

Hymns and prayers and shuffling and coughing, Perce reading the lesson and the magpies singing outside as if they knew it was a special day even for old Perce and had declared a truce.

While a prayer droned on, Paul listened to the noises beyond Mr Eversley's voice, the church's galvanised iron roof creaking and expanding its tired old joints in the sun, the wind throwing its gusty arms around the church as if it wanted to lift it bodily to heaven. There was the occasional shuffle of feet, the sudden roll of a dropped penny. And he wondered if the people were listening or whether their heads were full of worry about rain, soil and wheat prices or maybe just the war. He wished they'd hurry with the service. Ian gave a little restless movement in his mother's arms. But then the christening came and the baby was good.

"In the name of the Father and of the Son and of the Holy Ghost," said the Reverend Eversley, making a watery cross from the baptismal font on the baby's head. And Jody smiled and Paul saw Nancy take the baby back and he remembered John Grice and the little aeroplane and felt something deep inside him like tears, but it wasn't tears, he decided that it was some kind of happiness he hadn't experienced before.

Then came a sudden roar and everyone lifted their heads, and the CO smiled. Dead on time, he thought. Some people stood up to look out the church window and

116

saw the three small biplanes going over in formation in a salute. Flight Lieutenant Inster in the lead plane looked back at the church and gave a thumbs-up sign for the baby.

Mr Eversley nodded to Mrs Holifer who was so startled by the planes passing overhead that she pumped the organ furiously and all her fingers fell on the wrong keys, making the organ shriek with surprise. Ian gave a whisper.

And everyone stared at the organ, waiting for it to fall to pieces, but suddenly there came from it a deep and beautiful sound as if the organ had its own soul and had decided that, after all the dusty, unmelodious years of mistreatment it would make one last brave effort. A great look of contentment came over Mrs Holifer's face and she shut her eyes and played as if in Westminster Abbey itself.

A hymn, a benediction and then the church doors swung open and everyone streamed outside, clearing a path for Nancy and the baby, her mother, Aunt Rosa full of emotion and Jody and Paul following with Curtiss, DWO Wiles, while the CO and Perce brought up the rear.

There was a babble of talk, the baby had scores of admirers. Then Wing Commander Vines, the CO, said goodbye because his car had arrived. He saluted Nancy, shook her hand and admired the baby. He looked at the girl's steady eyes, with the dark lines under them. This is all part of it, he thought, young women and young men and all the futility and separation and sadness and yet a day like this, a hopeful day.

"I'm going overseas myself," he said, "on active service. Take care of yourself, Nancy. Everyone calls you

117

Nancy so may I too? As for you, Paul, you and Jody will get our official thanks for that quick wit of yours in saving one of our young men.''

They shook hands and the CO said to Paul: "And do remember me to your pig.''

The CO saluted again and was gone. So were DWO Wiles and Sergeant Hopson. The band and the men marched away to the waiting trucks.

"Mrs Moss," said Paul's mother, "would you come back for some tea?''

"Please," said Mrs Marchington Moss, "I would like to.''

Other people pressed forward for invitations.

"We'll never have enough cake," Paul said to Jody. He rather fancied the cake.

"Let's hope people don't start putting soap into the teapot again," Jody said.

That night after all the excitement, the talk, the emptying of teacups, the disappearing of cakes, more people coming with more cakes, people getting in each other's way in the kitchen, Aunt Rosa having to lie down in the spare room, Ian being described as "such a good child" by at least half the district, Curtiss pleased as punch and with his pipe glowing going off to feed the horses, with Perce accompanying him and both talking. . . . After it all, while Nancy and her mother were in the kitchen talking, Jody and Paul went to look at the baby. Jody had been allowed to stay the night, to help, so she said. But it was obvious that wasn't the only reason.

Ian's eyes were open. They caught the reflected light

118

from the next room, like small stars.

Suddenly, on an impulse, Paul lifted the baby from his cot.

"Let's come and see the stars, Ian," said Paul.

He tucked the blanket around Ian and carried him carefully to the verandah and sat on a low seat and Jody came and sat beside him.

It was a beautiful night. The stars swarmed like silver bees in the great hive of the sky and a thin young moon came over the nearby range.

Paul didn't hear a quick movement behind him. Then Nancy's voice quietly rebuking him. "You shouldn't take him from the crib without telling me, Tiger. He's had a big day. He's very tired."

"I brought him out to see the stars."

Nancy saw something in Paul's face. He's changing, she thought. He's growing up.

She looked away into the sky: "They are beautiful tonight. We seem closer to them."

An aeroplane engine coughed and roared over in a hangar where mechanics were working on it. The young woman and the girl and boy listened to it.

The wind stirred the old pepper tree into sleepy conversation.

Curtiss's words came back to Paul. "People die and people are born. Grass withers. New grass grows. . . ."

Paul felt the baby warm and alive move in his arms, and he felt older and more responsible.

"I don't think he wants to see the stars after all," he said. "I think he wants a feed."

THE HAMMERHEAD LIGHT

Colin Thiele

To Tessa Noble and the people of Snapper Bay the
Hammerhead Light was more than a lighthouse. It
was a symbol of all that was strong and enduring and
safe.

Tessa, growing up within sight and sound of the
Hammerhead, forms a deep bond with old Axel
Jorgenson, the lighthouse keeper. Then both their
lives are changed by a strange migratory bird, the
whimbrel, and Tessa learns the meaning of change
and the pain of growing up.

THE FIRE IN THE STONE

Colin Thiele

He picked up a small piece of stone and turned its
broken edge slowly in the light. Green, blue and
green, and a few needle-points of red. It was opal all
right – 'the fire in the stone'. For fourteen-year-old
Ernie Ryan, a dream had come true.

Living with his alcoholic father in a primitive
dugout in the harsh and lawless opal fields of inland
Australia, Ernie had either to fend for himself or
starve. But when his precious cache of opals is stolen
and he sets out with a friend determined to find the
thief, his dream becomes a series of nightmares.

THE CIRCUS RUNAWAYS

Margaret Pearce

Sawdust flying from the hooves of dancing horses,
glittering acrobats swinging high up on the trapeze,
fanfares and braided jackets – the excitement of the
circus was to turn a miserable winter into a season of
surprises for runaway John, his dog Blue and his horse
Roanie.

And life out of the circus ring was to be just as
eventful, for circus folk are different, wonderful,
funny . . . and sometimes dangerous.

Tallarook was only a short stop for the circus but it
was long enough for someone to try to burn the circus
down. Who could it be and why? As the days and
towns roll by, John finds out – not only about the
saboteur but also about growing up.

KING OF THE STICKS

Ivan Southall

There was a stillness and a listening – Custard could feel it all. He knew someone was spying on him, he could feel their eyes as he worked along the rows of beans. But who would believe him. They all thought he was vague, pixilated, dreamy . . .

Especially Seth. He always looked at Custard with a disappointment that this weedy kid was his brother. But Seth had gone to market and would not be home for two whole days.

Bella didn't have much faith in Custard either – but what else could you expect from a sister?

But Rebecca, his mother, did believe him. So she ventured forth, musket in hand, to face the enemy that threatened family and home.

So the day went crazy.

For Custard this was a beginning and not the end.

SALT RIVER TIMES

William Mayne

The Salt River runs through the inner-city suburb of
Iramoo; past the school and the park and the
warehouses. It also runs through these twenty-one
interlocking stories and through the lives of the people
who live and work in Iramoo – a gang of boys, an old
man with a steam engine, an elderly Chinese market
gardener, and a girl who throws stones.
   As the stories dovetail gently into each other the
intricate layers of the past are uncovered until an old
mystery of murder and treasure is solved.

HEARD ABOUT THE PUFFIN CLUB?

. . . it's a way of finding out more about Puffin books
and authors, of winning prizes (in competitions),
sharing jokes, a secret code, and perhaps seeing your
name in print! When you join you get a copy of our
magazine, *Puffinalia*, sent to you four times a year,
a badge and a membership book.
For details of subscription and an application form,
send a stamped addressed envelope to:

The Australian Puffin Club
Penguin Books Australia Limited
P.O. Box 257
Ringwood
Victoria 3134

and if you live in the UK, please write to

The Puffin Club Dept A
Penguin Books Limited
Bath Road
Harmondsworth
Middlesex UB7 ODA.